Short Stories: The Pedlar's Revenge

'This valuable collection displays O'Fla... ...
range from a love idyll b... ...
domestic duck to the u... ...
appalling Patsa, from the i... ...
splendid story "The Caress... ...

...edict Kiely

'This collection is a gallery of human emotions, embracing
a clutch of huge eccentrics, sweet and sour remembrances
of distant youth and vivid portraits of rural Ireland ... a
worthy representation of an unflinchingly lyric writer.'

The Sunday Times

Famine

'A major achievement – a masterpiece. The kind of truth
only a major writer of fiction is capable of portraying.'

Anthony Burgess

'The author's skill as a storyteller is at times breathtaking.
This is a most rewarding novel.'

Publishers Weekly

'A marvellously visual writer who prints his descriptions
on the retina.'

The Guardian

The Black Soul

'Embodies an energy that is genius.'

W. B. Yeats

'An elemental book because the primitive passions run free.'

AE

Skerrett

'One of the most powerful novels that this master-writer has ever produced.'

Irish Times

'Liam O'Flaherty is a great, great writer whose work must be unique in any language, any culture. He has all the potential for becoming a matrix for the yearnings of another generation.'

Neil Jordan

'Powerful in language, majestic in scope, utterly honest.'

Sunday Press

The Wilderness

'*The Wilderness* is essentially a simple story of unbridled passions, frustrated ambitions and hunger for land, but in the hands of O'Flaherty it becomes a *tour de force* that tears through the mind with the careless abandon of an Atlantic breaker.'

Sunday Press

LIAM O'FLAHERTY

Born in 1896 on Inishmore, the largest of the Aran Islands, Liam O'Flaherty grew up in a world of awesome beauty, echoes from his descendants and the ancient pagan past. From his father, a Fenian, O'Flaherty inherited a rebellious streak; from his mother, a noted *seanchaí* (storyteller), came the deep spiritualism and love of nature that has enraptured readers through the decades.

In France in 1917 O'Flaherty was severely shell-shocked. After a short recuperation, he spent several restless years travelling the globe. In 1920 he supported the Republican cause against the Free State government. Influenced by the Industrial Workers of the World's programme of social revolution, O'Flaherty organised the seizure and occupation of the Rotunda Theatre at the top of Dublin's O'Connell Street in 1922. He hoisted the red flag of revolution, calling himself the 'Chairman of the Council of the Unemployed', but fled three days later to avoid bloodshed. Later that year he moved to London, where his writing skills came to the attention of critic Edward Garnett, who recommended to Jonathan Cape the publication of O'Flaherty's first novel. For the next two decades, O'Flaherty's creative output was astonishing. Writing in English and Irish, he produced novels, memoirs and short stories by the dozen. Remarkable for their literary value and entertainment, O'Flaherty's books are also crucial from an anthropological point of view, charting the ways and beliefs of a peasant world before it was eclipsed by modernity.

Some of O'Flaherty's work was banned in Ireland – he was a rebel in his writing, as in his life. Liam O'Flaherty died in Dublin in 1984, aged 88 years, having enriched forever Irish literature and culture.

To Kitty

Other books by LIAM O'FLAHERTY
available from WOLFHOUND PRESS

FICTION
Famine
Short Stories: The Pedlar's Revenge
The Wilderness
Skerrett
Insurrection
The Assassin
Mr. Gilhooley
The Ecstasy of Angus

AUTOBIOGRAPHY
Shame the Devil

FOR CHILDREN
The Test of Courage
All Things Come of Age

FORTHCOMING
The Letters of Liam O'Flaherty
(Edited by A. A. Kelly)

LIAM O'FLAHERTY

the pedlar's revenge

short stories

Selected and introduced by A. A. Kelly

WOLFHOUND PRESS

New edition, 1996
WOLFHOUND PRESS Ltd
68 Mountjoy Square
Dublin 1

Reprinted 1996, 1999

Wolfhound Press (UK)
18 Coleswood Rd
Harpenden
Herts AL5 1EQ

Published in paperback 1982, 1986, 1989, 1991, 1993
© 1976 Liam O'Flaherty
Introduction © A. A. Kelly

All rights reserved. No part of this book may be reproduced or utilised in any form or by any means digital, electronic or mechanical including photography, filming, recording, video recording, photocopying, or by any information storage and retrieval system or shall not, by way of trade or otherwise, be lent, resold or otherwise circulated in any form of binding or cover other than that in which it is published without prior permission in writing from the publisher.

First published 1976
by Wolfhound Press Ltd

Wolfhound Press receives financial assistance from the Arts Council/
An Chomhairle Ealaíon, Dublin.

British Library Cataloguing in Publication Data
A catalogue record for this book is available from the British Library.

ISBN 0-86327-536-2

Typesetting: Wolfhound Press
Cover illustration and design: Jon Berkeley
Printed by The Guernsey Press Co. Ltd., Guernsey.

CONTENTS

Acknowledgements

Many of these stories first appeared in the magazines or journals acknowledged here: 'The Salted Goat' in *The Irish Statesman*, 'The White Bitch' in *The Weekly Westminster*, 'A Crow Fight' in *The Dublin Magazine*, 'Fishing' in *The Irish Statesman* (1924); 'A Tin Can' and 'The Arrest' in *The Weekly Westminster*, 'The Flood' in *The Dublin Magazine* (1925); 'Patsa, or The Belly of Gold' in *The London Aphrodite*, 1928; 'The Mermaid' in *John-O London's Weekly*, 1929; 'Lovers' in *Harper's*, 'The Proclamation' in *The Yale Review* (1931); 'The Caress' in O'Flaherty's autobiographical volume, *Shame the Devil*, 1934; 'All things come of age' in *Esquire*, 'King of Inishcam' as Irish Pride in *Forum* (1935); 'The Test of Courage' in *Esquire*, 1943; 'Timoney's Ass' as 'A matter of Freedom' in *Tomorrow Magazine*, 1947; 'The Pedlar's Revenge' in *The Bell*, 1952; 'The Enchanted Water' in *The Yale Review*, 1952; 'The Fanatic' in *The Bell*, 1953. 'Wild Stallions' and 'Bohunk' appear in print for the first time in this collection.

INTRODUCTION

Liam O'Flaherty belongs to the same Irish writer vintage as Frank O'Connor, Sean O'Faolain, Francis Stuart and Austin Clarke, all of whom grew to manhood before Ireland gained her independence. Unlike these others he was born on Inishmore, Aran Islands; raised in a bi-lingual Irish-English community where life was a struggle against the elements and poverty, and where oral story-telling still took place round the fire on long winter nights. Courage was an inbred quality for survival on Aran. Physical and moral courage remains O'Flaherty's most admired human attribute.

His feeling for language, enriched by the early possession of two such different tongues and the sonorities of the Latin Mass, was brought to a finer awareness by reading the classics. In 1915 the spirit of adventure led him to leave University College Dublin, to drop Catullus — still his favourite classical author — and enrol in the Irish Guards. The Easter Rebellion found him in France, experiencing the bloodbath of World War I trench warfare, horrors still vivid in his powerful visual memory. In 1917 he was shell-shocked, wounded and discharged. His subsequent adventures roaming the world he later wrote about in *Two Years* (1930).

Though O'Flaherty's first story to arouse attention, 'The Sniper' (1923), is set in the Irish civil war of the previous year in which he had taken part as a republican, only two of his fourteen novels published between 1923 and 1950 treat of warfare, and only four of his one hundred and fifty short stories. His first short story collection, *Spring Sowing* (1924), showed he could write lyrically of man and beast in natural surroundings, but a liking for struggle, an undercurrent of violence, remains an important characteristic of his work.

Man — like the sea — can be malign, benign, or suddenly erupt from one state to the other. This kindred feeling for the moods of nature, and their response in man, pervades much of his work and his writing can be charged with either lyrical gentleness or callous brutality. Feelings are strong — 'frenzy' and 'ecstasy' are two of his favoured words.

The following passage from his little known second novel, *The Black Soul* (1924), set in Inverara (fictional Aran), illustrates his heritage:

The people feared the resting bilious sea as a soldier fears the silence of the guns in an interval between two engagements. When it raged, churned by the wind, it showed its might, but now the huge claws of its breakers were hidden in its frothing back. And they might shoot forth any moment. The sea might rise suddenly far away to the west and come towering in, each forked wave-crest a magnet, that drew the sea before it into its hollow breast, until the Giants' Reef lay bared for a mile and the slimy insects clinging to its back stared gasping at the awe-inspiring sky before the retreating sea again enveloped them in accustomed darkness. For the battle is not as fearsome as the waiting for it, nor is the sword as terrible as the fire in the eye that guides it. So the peasants feared the sea, and fearing it blessed it as their generous mother, who wrecked ships afar off to give them planks and barrels of oil and manila ropes and bales of cotton. They prowled about the shores and among the boulders beneath the Hill of Fate looking for wreckage.

By day the sun shone fitfully on Rooruck coming laggardly over the high cliff of Coillnamham Fort. Its shadows glistened through the mist and through the clouds that pursued it. By night the hoar-frost covered the earth, eating into the gashes that the wind had made. Wild starry nights were those nights in Inverara. Boys sat by their windows, shivering in their shirts afraid to sleep because of the strange noises of falling seas that came from the Fountain Hole, where the mermaids were said to weep for lost lovers as they combed their long golden hair, dipping the combs in the black brine that dripped from the roof of their cave into the Purple Pool beneath. Wild starry nights, when men dream of death and stillness, as they watch the shivering moon fleeing through the scratched sky. Death, death, death, and drear winds blowing around frozen dead hearts, that once throbbed with love. Inverara in winter is the island of death, the island of defeated peoples, come thither through the ages over the sea pursued by their enemies. Their children sit on the cliffs dreaming of the past of their fathers, dreaming of the sea, the wind, the moon, the stars, the scattered remnants of an army, the remains of a feast eaten by dogs, the shattering of a maniac's ambition.

Fear and the overcoming of it, acceptance of death, struggle against physical and moral defeat, fertility

won hard from the soil and sea, escape into the story-
land of past dreams, of myth and legend, O'Flaherty
the dreamy poet and O'Flaherty the sarcastic realist
— all are here expressed.

Five collections of O'Flaherty short stories in English
were published between 1924 and 1948, one collection
in Irish in 1953, and six new stories were included in
a 1956 American selection of previously collected work.
This volume gathers together some uncollected and
unpublished stories written between 1923 and the
1960s. No attempt has been made to arrange the stories
in chronological order of composition. Each should
be enjoyed for what it is. All but three stories have been
published previously in magazines and journals; 'The
Caress' formed a coda to O'Flaherty's second autobiographical volume, *Shame the Devil* (1934), and here
appears as a short story in its own right for the first
time, two previously unpublished stories are 'Bohunk'
and 'Wild Stallions'.

Although O'Flaherty uses a wide range of subject
matter the careful reader will remark certain predom-
inant genres and themes. Animal and nature stories,
for which he is justly famous, are represented here
by 'All things come of age' and 'A Crow Fight', in both
of which the parent protects its young. Nature is not
sentimental, the violence of predator and prey, or rival
factions within a species, as in 'Wild Stallions', are often
the subject of these simply written tales which illustrate the frenetic urge to perpetuate the species against
threat from outside. Survival as an instinct in living
things is shown even more clearly in 'The Flood'. The
minutest insects fight for life. Their remainder is compared collectively to a 'horde' or a 'rash' on the earth's
surface.

'The Enchanted Water', like many O'Flaherty stories

set on Aran or in western Ireland, is imbued with the mystery of place. It takes us into the body of the community, the 'our village' of which the old fisherman narrator is a member. For him 'there is a grain of truth in everything that's handed down from ancient times'. The gentle treatment of the wild duckling here contrasts vividly with the tortured goat mentioned in 'Patsa, or the belly of gold'. This last story, as explicit as parts of Chaucer — with its gibes at Celtic twilight and amusing portrait of Patsa of the chancred nose and filthy ears, is typical of O'Flaherty's abrasive humour in which comic farce and tragedy often intertwine. Yet the same man could write 'The Mermaid' a few months later.

The myth and superstitions so alive in the minds of these Aran and western people often form the basis of emotional response as in 'The Salted Goat' and 'The Mermaid'. Behind the language of such peasant stories echoes generations of oral tradition in which pagan myth and Christian habit mingle so that when Margaret Conroy dies, 'Wise old women that followed her corpse to the grave said that a convent was the proper place for such frail beauty; that it could only live wedded to the gentle Christ. Others, who still believed in the ancient sorceries, said that the God Crom had taken her for his bride'.

Much of O'Flaherty's Aran writings draw on personal experience, a memory of something he heard as a child, a memory of real people he knew as in 'A Tin Can'; or a real scene which he peoples with fictionalised characters in a known situation as in 'Fishing' and 'Timoney's Ass' — both reminiscent of other stories he has written in the same vein.

To O'Flaherty's occasional stories about children, such as 'A New Suit' and 'The Wren's Nest', can now be added 'The Test of Courage' which not only illustrates the importance he attaches to this quality, but also introduces another sea story to old favourites like

'The Landing' and 'The Oar'.

In O'Flaherty's characters misplaced idealism or illusions about themselves may give rise to obsessions of revenge, possessiveness, or fear, centred on another person, animal or object — a woman, a goat or a piece of gold. In their single-mindedness these characters are all tinged by a fanatic tenacity which the world labels queer, or absurd, because it does not conform to the pattern of accepted social behaviour. O'Flaherty enjoys writing about off-beat characters like Patsa, and the protagonists of 'The Fanatic' and 'The Pedlar's Revenge'. Some of the drunks in his stories are high on more than alcohol. They pass through a fleetingly perceptive exaltation though they may end up helpless over a horse's back.

Racy storyteller, lyrical poet, caustic social commentator, these contradictory critical 'labels' could all be attached to O'Flaherty. Evasive of publicity he has never sought fuller recognition. Much of his longer work, either because of the satiric or melodramatic vein which pervades it, has not been sufficiently appreciated, and to some of his contemporaries it cut too near the bone. Less controversial, more appealing, his lyrical short stories received immediate recognition. But in addition to writing sensitive nature stories, O'Flaherty's story-telling chronicles an Irish peasant community life which has now changed. A shrewd outspoken observer of the political and social foibles of humanity, his work at times challenges protest in delicate areas of concern.

Nothing is sacrosanct to O'Flaherty except — as with all artists — his own inner self. All art must come from the inner contradictions of the artist which continue to present themselves in endless succession like humpbacked waves drawn up by the moon of his perpetual quest. The true artist is incapable of revealing himself fully because the deep philosophic analysis necessary for this would impoverish the seedbed of intuitive impulse upon which his creative hunger feeds. The reader can only hope to gain glimpses or hints by which to get nearer to this inner self in order to appreciate the work more fully.

O'Flaherty once said:

There are some writers whom one immediately recognises, bookish fellows, whose drawing room civilisation obtrudes unpleasantly on the senses. They are just writers, no matter how great. But there are others who are great men, because they are men and who write because chance turns their energies towards writing as a means of creation. These are the men I love. Out of their speech, out of their eyes, out of the movements of their bodies, joyousness and exuberance flow and they make you feel that it is good to be alive . . . . Critics do not know what to make of their work; and only when they are dead do the critics come from the caves, where they have been hiding from the hurricane of genius, to write scholarly dissertations on the beauty of the hurricane that has passed, having wasted its beautiful frenzy.

This passage might have been written about himself.

A. A. Kelly

THE PEDLAR'S REVENGE

Old Paddy Moynihan was dead when the police appeared on the scene of the accident. He lay stretched out on his back at the bottom of the deep ravine below the blacksmith's house. His head rested on a smooth round granite stone and his hands were crossed over his enormous stomach. His battered old black hat was tied onto his skull with a piece of twine that passed beneath his chin. Men and boys from the village stood around him in a circle, discussing the manner of his death in subdued tones. Directly overhead, women and girls leaned in a compact group over the low stone wall of the blacksmith's yard. They were all peering down into the shadowy depths of the ravine at the dim shape of the dead man, with their mouths wide open and a fixed look of horror in their eyes.

Sergeant Toomey made a brief inspection of the corpse and then turned to Joe Finnerty, the rate collector.

'Tommy Murtagh told me,' he said, 'that it was you...'

'Yes,' said Finnerty. 'It was I sent Tommy along to fetch you. I told him to get a priest as well, but no priest came.'

'Both the parish priest and the curate are away on

sick calls at the moment,' said the sergeant.

'In any case,' said Finnerty, 'there was little that a priest could do for him. The poor old fellow remained unconscious from the moment he fell until he died.'

'Did you see him fall?' said the sergeant.

'I did,' said Finnerty. 'I was coming down the road when I caught sight of him on the blacksmith's wall there above. He was very excited. He kept shouting and brandishing his stick. "The Pedlar poisoned me," he said. He kept repeating that statement in a sing-song shout, over and over again, like a whinging child. Then he got to his feet and moved forward, heading for the road. He had taken only half a step, though, when he seemed to get struck by some sort of colic. He dropped his stick, clutched his stomach with both hands and staggered backwards, bent almost double, to sit down again on the wall. The next thing I knew, he was going head over heels into the ravine, backwards, yelling like a stuck pig. Upon my soul! His roaring must have been heard miles away.'

'It was a terrific yell, all right,' said Peter Lavin, the doctor's servant. 'I was mowing down there below in the meadow when I heard it. I raised my head like a shot and saw old Paddy go through the air. Great God! He looked as big as a house. He turned somersault twice before he passed out of my sight, going on away down into the hole. I heard the splash, though, when he struck the ground, like a heavy sack dropped into the sea from a boat's deck.'

He pointed towards a deep wide dent in the wet ground to the right and said:

'That was where he landed, sergeant.'

The sergeant walked over and looked at the hollow. The whole ground was heavily laden with water that flowed from the mossy face of the cliff. Three little boys had stuck a rolled dock-leaf into a crevice and they were drinking in turn at the thin jet of water that came from the bright green funnel.

'Why did he think he was poisoned?' said the sergeant.

'I've no idea,' said Finnerty. 'It's certain, in any case, that he had swallowed something that didn't agree with him. The poor fellow was in convulsions with pain just before he fell.'

The sergeant looked up along the sheer face of the cliff at a thick cluster of ivy that grew just beneath the overarching brow. A clutch of young sparrows were chirping plaintively for food from their nest within the ivy.

'According to him,' the sergeant said, as he walked back to the corpse, 'The Pedlar was responsible for whatever ailed him.'

'That's right,' said Finnerty. 'He kept repeating that The Pedlar had poisoned him, over and over again. I wouldn't pay much attention to that, though, The Pedlar and himself were deadly enemies. They have accused one another of every crime in the calendar scores of times.'

' 'Faith, I saw him coming out of The Pedlar's house a few hours ago,' said Anthony Gill. 'He didn't look like a poisoned man at that time. He had a broad smile on his face and he was talking to himself, as he came shuffling down along the road towards me. I asked him where he was going in such a great hurry and he told me to mind my own business. I looked back after he had passed and saw him go into Pete Maloney's shop.'

'I was there when he came in,' said Bartly Timoney. 'He was looking for candles.'

'Candles?' said the sergeant.

'He bought four candles,' Timoney said. 'He practically ran out of the shop with them, mumbling to himself and laughing. Begob, like Anthony there said, he seemed to be in great form at the time.'

'Candles?' said the sergeant again. 'Why should he be in such a great hurry to buy candles?'

'Poor man!' said Finnerty. 'He was very old and not quite right in the head. Lord have mercy on him, he's been half-mad these last two years, ever since he lost his wife. Ah! The poor old fellow is better off dead than the way he was, living all alone in his little cottage, without anybody to feed him and keep him clean.'

The sergeant turned to Peter Lavin and said:

'Did the doctor come back from town yet?'

'He won't be back until this evening,' Lavin said. 'He's waiting over for the result of the operation on Tom Kelly's wife.'

'All right, lads,' the sergeant said. 'We might as well see about removing poor old Moynihan.'

'That's easier said than done,' said Anthony Gill. 'We weighed him a few weeks ago in Quinn's scales against three sacks of flour to settle a bet. Charley Ridge, the lighthouse keeper, bet a pound note that he was heavier than three sacks of flour and Tommy Perkins covered the pound, maintaining that he would fall short of that weight. The lighthouse keeper lost, but it was only by a whisker. I never saw anything go so close. There were only a few ounces in the difference. Well! Three sacks of flour weigh three hundred and thirty-six pounds. How are we going to carry that much dead weight out of this hole?'

'The simplest way, sergeant,' said Guard Hynes, 'would be to get a rope and haul him straight up to the blacksmith's yard.'

Everybody agreed with Hynes.

'I've got a lot of gear belonging to my boat up at the house,' said Bartly Timoney. 'I'll go and get a strong rope.'

He began to clamber up the side of the ravine.

'Bring a couple of slings as well,' the sergeant called after him. 'They'll keep him steady.'

All the younger men followed Timoney, in order to give a hand with the hauling.

'There may be heavier men than old Moynihan,' said Finnerty to those that remained below with the corpse, 'but he was the tallest and the strongest man seen in this part of the country within living memory. He was six feet ten inches in his bare feet and there was no known limit to his strength. I've seen him toss a full-grown bullock without hardly any effort at all, in the field behind Tom Daly's pub at Gortmor. Then he drank the three gallons of porter that he won for doing it, as quickly as you or I would drink three pints.'

'He was a strong man, all right,' said Gill. 'You could heap a horse's load onto his back and he'd walk away with it, as straight as a rod, calmly smoking his pipe.'

'Yet he was as gentle as a child,' said Lavin, 'in spite of his strength. They say that he never struck anybody in his whole life.'

'Many is the day he worked on my land,' said Sam Clancy, 'and I'll agree that he was as good as ten men. He could keep going from morning to night without slackening pace. However, it was the devil's own job giving him enough to eat. The side of a pig, or even a whole sheep, would make no more than a good snack for him. The poor fellow told me that he suffered agonies from hunger. He could never get enough to eat. It must have been absolute torture for him, when he got too old to work and had to live on the pension.'

Timoney came back and threw down two slings, over the low wall where the women and girls were gathered. Then he let down the end of a stout rope. Sergeant Toomey made one sling fast about Moynihan's upper chest and the other about his knees. Then he passed the end of the rope through the slings and knotted it securely.

'Haul away now,' he said to Timoney.

The two old sparrows fluttered back and forth across

the ravine, uttering shrill cries, when they saw the corpse drawn up slowly along the face of the cliff. The fledgings remained silent in obedience to these constantly repeated warnings, until old Moynihan's dangling right hand brushed gently against the ivy outside their nest. The light sound being like that made by the bodies of their parents, when entering with food, they broke into a frenzied chatter. Thereupon, the old birds became hysterical with anxiety. The mother dropped a piece of worm from her beak. Then she and her cock hurled themselves at old Moynihan's head, with all their feathers raised. They kept attacking him fiercely, with beak and claw, until he was drawn up over the wall into the yard.

When the corpse was stretched out on the black-smith's cart, Sergeant Toomey turned to the women that were there and said:

'It would be an act of charity for ye to come and get him ready for burial. He has nobody of his own to wash and shave him.'

'In God's name,' they said, 'We'll do whatever is needed.'

They all followed the men that were pushing the cart up the road towards the dead man's cottage.

'Listen,' the sergeant said to Finnerty, as they walked along side by side. 'Didn't The Pedlar bring old Moynihan to court at one time over the destruction of a shed.'

'He did, 'faith,' said Finnerty, 'and he was awarded damages, too, by District Justice Roche.'

'How long ago was that?' the sergeant said.

'It must be over twenty years,' said Finnerty.

'A long time before I came here,' said the sergeant. 'I never heard the proper details of the story.'

'It was only a ramshackle old shed,' said Finnerty, 'where The Pedlar used to keep all the stuff that he collected around the countryside, rags and old iron and bits of ancient furniture and all sorts of curiosities that had been washed ashore from wrecked ships. Moynihan came along one day and saw The Pedlar's ass tied to the iron staple in the door-jamb of the shed. Lord have mercy on the dead, he was very fond of playing childish pranks, like all simple-minded big fellows. So he got a turnip and stuck it onto the end of his stick. Then he leaned over the wall of The Pedlar's backyard and began to torment the ass, drawing the unfortunate animal on and on after the turnip. The ass kept straining at its rope until the door-jamb was dragged out of the wall. Then the wall collapsed and finally the whole shed came down in a heap. The Pedlar was away at the time and nobody saw the damage being done except old Moynihan himself. The poor fellow would have got into no trouble if he had kept his mouth shut. Instead of doing so, it was how he ran down into the village and told everybody what had happened. He nearly split his sides laughing at his own story. As a result of his confessions, he very naturally didn't have a foot to stand on when the case came up before the court.'

The dead man's cottage looked very desolate. The little garden in front was overgrown with weeds. There were several large holes in the roof. The door was broken. The windows were covered with sacking. The interior was in a shocking state of filth and disorder.

'He'll have to stay on the cart,' said Sergeant Toomey, after he had inspected the two rooms, 'until there is a proper place to lay him out like a christian.'

He left Guard Hynes in charge of the body and then set off with Joe Finnerty to The Pedlar's cottage.

'I couldn't find the candles,' he said on the way. 'Neither could I find out exactly what he had for his last meal. His little pot and his frying pan were on the hearth, having evidently been used to prepare whatever he ate. There was a small piece of potato skin at the bottom of the pot, but the frying pan was licked as clean as a new pin. God only knows what he fried on it.'

'Poor old Paddy!' said Finnerty. 'He had been half-starved for a long time. He was going around like a dog, scavenging for miserable scraps in shameful places. Yet people gave him sufficient food to satisfy the appetite of any ordinary person, in addition to what he was able to buy with his pension money.'

The Pedlar's cottage was only a few yards away from Moynihan's sordid hovel, to which its neatness offered a very striking contrast. It was really very pretty, with its windows painted dark blue and its walls spotlessly white and the bright May sunlight sparkling on its slate roof. The garden was well stocked with fruit trees and vegetables and flowers, all dressed in a manner that bore evidence to the owner's constant diligence and skill. It also contained three hives of honey-bees which made a pleasant clamour as they worked among the flowers. The air was charged with a delicious perfume, which was carried up by the gentle breeze from the different plants and flowers.

The Pedlar hailed the two men as they were approaching the house along a narrow flagged path that ran through the centre of the garden.

'Good day,' he said to them. 'What's goin' on over at Paddy Moynihan's house? I heard a cart and a lot of people arrive there.'

He was sitting on a three-legged stool to the right of the open door-way. His palsied hands moved up and down, constantly, along the blackthorn stick that he held erect between his knees. His legs were also palsied. The metalled heels of his boots kept beating a minute and almost inaudible tattoo on the broad smooth flag-stone beneath his stool. He was very small and so stooped that he was bent almost double. His boots, his threadbare black suit, his white shirt and his black felt hat were all very neat; like his house and his garden. Indeed, he was immaculately clean from head to foot, except for his wrinkled little face. It was in great part covered with stubbly grey hair, that looked more like an animal's fur than a proper human beard.

'It was old Paddy Moynihan himself,' said the sergeant in a solemn tone, 'that they brought home on the cart.'

The Pedlar laughed drily in his throat, making a sound that was somewhat like the bleating of a goat, plaintive and without any merriment.

'Ho! Ho! Did the shameless scoundrel get drunk again?' he said in a thin high-pitched voice. 'Two months ago, he got speechless in Richie Tallon's pub with two sheep-jobbers from Castlegorm. He had to be taken home on Phil Manion's ass-cart. There wasn't room for the whole of him on the cart. Two lads had to follow along behind, holding up the lower parts of his legs.'

'Old Paddy is dead,' the sergeant said in a stern tone.

The Pedlar became motionless for a few moments on hearing this news, with his shrewd blue eyes looking upwards at the sergeant's face from beneath his bushy grey eyebrows. Then his heels began once more to beat their minute tattoo and his fingers moved tremulously along the surface of the blackthorn stick, up and down, as if it were a pipe from which they were drawing music.

'I'll ask God to have mercy on his soul,' he said coldly, 'but I won't say that I'm sorry to hear he's dead. Why should I? To tell you the honest truth, the news that you bring lifts a great weight off my mind. How did he die?'

He again laughed drily in his throat, after the sergeant had told him the manner of old Moynihan's death. His laughter now sounded gay.

'It must have been his weight that killed him,' he said, 'for John Delaney, a carpenter that used to live in

Srulane long ago, fell down at that very same place
without hurting himself in the least. It was a terrible
night, about forty years ago. Delaney was coming home
alone from a funeral at Tirnee, where he had gone to
make the coffin. As usual, he was dead drunk, and never
let a word out of him as he fell. He stayed down there
in the hole for the rest of that night and all next day. He
crawled out of it at nightfall, as right as rain. That same
Delaney was the king of all drunkards. I remember one
time he fell into a coffin he was making for an old
woman at...'

'I must warn you,' Sergeant Toomey interrupted,
'that Paddy Moynihan made certain allegations against
you, in the presence of Joe Finnerty here, shortly
before he died. They were to the effect that you had...'

'Ho! Ho! Bad cess to the scoundrel!' The Pedlar
interrupted in turn. 'He's been making allegations
against me all his life. He's been tormenting me, too.
God forgive me! I've hated that man since I was a child.'

'You've hated him all that time?' said the sergeant.

'We were the same age,' said The Pedlar. 'I'll be
seventy-nine next month. I'm only a few weeks older
than Paddy. We started going to school on the very
same day. He took a violent dislike to me from the first
moment he laid eyes on me. I was born stooped, just the
same as I am now. I was delicate into the bargain and
they didn't think I'd live. When I was seven or eight
years old, I was no bigger than a dwarf. On the other
hand, Paddy Moynihan was already a big hefty block
of a lad. He was twice the size of other boys his own
age. He tortured me in every way that he could. His
favourite trick was to sneak up behind me and yell into
my ear. You know what a powerful voice he had as a
grown man. Well! It was very nearly as powerful when
he was a lad. His yell was deep and rumbling, like the
roar of an angry bull. I always fell down in a fit whenever he sneaked up behind me and yelled into my ear.'

'That was no way to treat a delicate lad,' said the sergeant in a sympathetic tone. 'It was no wonder that you got to hate him.'

'Don't believe a word of what he's telling you,' said Finnerty to the sergeant. 'Paddy Moynihan never did anything of the sort.'

The Pedlar again became motionless for a few seconds, as he looked at Finnerty's legs. Then he resumed his dance and turned his glance back to the sergeant's face.

'He did worse things to me,' he said. 'He made the other scholars stand around me in a ring and beat my bare feet with little pebbles. He used to laugh at the top of his voice while he watched them do it. If I tried to break out of the ring, or sat down on the ground and put my feet under me, he'd threaten me with worse torture. "Stand there," he'd say, "or I'll keep shouting into your ear until you die." Of course, I'd rather let them go on beating me than have him do the other thing. Oh! God! The shouting in my ear was a terrible torture. I used to froth at the mouth so much, when I fell down, that they thought for a long time I had epilepsy.'

'You old devil!' cried Finnerty angrily. 'You should be ashamed of yourself for telling lies about the dead.'

'Let him have his say,' the sergeant said to Finnerty. 'Every man has a right to say what he pleases on his own threshold.'

'He had no right to speak ill of the dead, all the same,' said Finnerty, 'especially when there isn't a word of truth in what he says. Sure, it's well known that poor old Paddy Moynihan, Lord have mercy on him, wouldn't hurt a fly. There was no more harm in him than in a babe unborn.'

'Take it easy, Joe,' said the sergeant. 'There are two sides to every story.'

Then he turned to The Pedlar and added:

' 'Faith, you had cause to hate Moynihan, all right.

No wonder you planned to get revenge on him.'

'I was too much afraid of him at that time,' said The Pedlar, 'to think of revenge. Oh! God! He had the life nearly frightened out of me. He and his gang used to hunt me all the way home from school, throwing little stones at me and clods of dirt. "Pedlar, Pedlar, Pedlar," they'd shout and they coming after me.'

'Musha, bad luck to you,' said Finnerty, 'for a cunning old rascal, trying to make us believe it was Paddy Moynihan put the scholars up to shouting "Pedlar" after you. Sure, everybody in the parish has shouted "Pedlar" after a Counihan at one time or other and thought nothing of it. Neither did the Counihans. Why should they? They've all been known as "The Pedlars" from one generation to another, every mother's son of them.'

The sergeant walked over to the open doorway and thrust his head into the kitchen.

'Leave the man alone,' he said to Finnerty.

The fireplace, the dressers that were laden with beautiful old brown delft-ware and the flagged floor were all spotlessly clean and brightly polished.

'Ah! Woe!' The Pedlar cried out in a loud voice, as he began to rock himself like a lamenting woman. 'The Counihans are all gone except myself and I'll soon be gone, too, leaving no kith or kin behind me. The day of the wandering merchant is now done. He and his ass will climb no more up from the sea along the stony mountain roads, bringing lovely bright things from faraway cities to the wild people of the glens. Ah! Woe! Woe!'

'If you were that much afraid of Moynihan,' said the sergeant, as he walked back from the doorway to The Pedlar's stool, 'it must have been the devil's own job for you to get revenge on him.'

The Pedlar stopped rocking himself and looked up sideways at the sergeant, with a very cunning smile on his little bearded face.

'It was easy,' he whispered in a tone of intense pleasure, 'once I had learned his secret.'

'What secret did he have?' said the sergeant.

'He was a coward,' said The Pedlar.

'A coward!' cried Finnerty. 'Paddy Moynihan a coward!'

'Keep quiet, Joe,' said the sergeant.

'I was nineteen years of age at the time,' said The Pedlar, 'and in such a poor state of health that I was barely able to walk. Yet I had to keep going. My mother, Lord have mercy on her, had just died after a long sickness, leaving me alone in the world with hardly a penny to my name. I was coming home one evening from Ballymullen, with a load of goods in my ass's creels, when Moynihan came along and began to torment me. "Your load isn't properly balanced," he said. "It's going to overturn." Then he began to pick up loose stones from the road and put them into the creels, first into one and then into the other, pretending that he was trying to balance the load. I knew very well what he had in mind, but I said nothing. I was speechless with fright. Then he suddenly began to laugh and he took bigger stones from the wall and threw them into the creels, one after the other. Laughing at the top of his voice, he kept throwing in more and more stones, until the poor ass fell down under the terrible weight. That was more than I could bear. In spite of my terror, I picked up a stone and threw it at him. It wasn't much of a stone and I didn't throw it hard, but it struck him in the cheek and managed to draw blood. He put up his hand and felt the cut. Then he looked at his fingers. "Lord God!" he said in a weak little voice. "Blood is coming from my cheek. I'm cut." Upon my soul, he let a terrible yell out of him and set off down the road towards the village as fast as he could, with his hand to his cheek and he screaming like a frightened girl.

As for me, 'faith, I raised up my ass and went home happy that evening. There was a little bird singing in my heart, for I knew that Moynihan would never again be able to torture me.'

'Right enough,' said the sergeant, 'you had him in your power after that. You had only to decide...'

'Best of all, though,' The Pedlar interrupted excitedly, 'was when I found out that he was mortally afraid of bees. Before that, he was able to steal all my fruit and vegetables while I was out on the roads. It was no use keeping a dog. The sight of him struck terror into the fiercest dog there ever was.'

'You wicked old black spider!' said Finnerty. 'Why do you go on telling lies about the dead?'

'Keep quiet, Joe,' said the sergeant. 'Let him finish his story!'

'All animals loved Moynihan,' said Finnerty, 'because he was gentle with them. They knew there was no harm in him. Children loved him, too. Indeed, every living creature was fond of the poor old fellow except this vindictive little cripple, who envied his strength and his good nature and his laughter. It was his rollicking laughter, above all else, that aroused the hatred of this cursed little man.'

'So you got bees,' the sergeant said to The Pedlar.

'I bought three hives,' The Pedlar said, 'and put them here in the garden. That did the trick. Ho! Ho! The ruffian has suffered agonies on account of those bees, especially since the war made food scarce in the shops. Many is the good day's sport I've had, sitting here on my stool, watching him go back and forth like a hungry wolf, with his eyes fixed on the lovely fruit and vegetables that he daren't touch. Even so, I'm glad to hear he's dead.'

'You are?' said Sergeant Toomey.

'It takes a load off my mind,' The Pedlar said.

'It does?' said the sergeant.

'Lately,' said The Pedlar, 'I was beginning to get afraid of him again. He was going mad with hunger. You can't trust a madman. In spite of his cowardice, he might attack me in order to rob my house and garden.'

'Was that why you decided to poison him?' said the sergeant.

The Pedlar started violently and became motionless, with his upward-glancing eyes fixed on the sergeant's chest. He looked worried for a moment. Then his bearded face became suffused with a cunning smile and his palsied limbs resumed their uncouth dance. The metalled heels of his boots now made quite a loud and triumphant sound as they beat upon the flagstone.

'You are a clever man, Sergeant Toomey,' he whispered in a sneering tone, 'but you'll never be able to prove that I'm guilty of having caused Paddy Moynihan's death.'

'He was in your house to-day,' said the sergeant.

'He was,' said The Pedlar.

'Did you give him anything?' said the sergeant.

'I gave him nothing,' said The Pedlar.

'You might as well tell the truth,' said the sergeant. 'When the doctor comes back this evening, we'll know exactly what old Moynihan had for his last meal.'

'I can tell you that myself,' said The Pedlar.

'You can?' said the sergeant.

'He burst into my kitchen,' said The Pedlar, 'while I was frying a few potatoes with some of the bacon fat that I collect in a bowl. "Where did you get the bacon?" he said. He loved bacon and he was furious because there was none to be had in the shops. "I have no bacon," I said. "You're a liar," said he. "I can smell it." I was afraid to tell him the truth, for fear he might ransack the house and find my bowl of bacon fat. Then he'd kill me if I tried to prevent him from marching off with it. So I told him it was candles I was frying with the potatoes. God forgive me, I was terribly frightened by the wild look in his eyes. So I told him the first thing that came into my head, in order to get him out of the house. "Candles!" he said. "In that case, I'll soon be eating fried potatoes myself." Then he ran out of the house. I locked the door as soon as he had gone. Not long afterwards, he came back and tried to get in, but I pretended not to hear him knocking. "You old miser!" he shouted, as he gave the door a terrible kick that nearly took it off its hinges. "I have candles myself now. I'll soon be as well fed as you are." He kept laughing to himself as he went away. That was the last I saw or heard of him.'

'You think he ate the candles?' said the sergeant.

'I'm certain of it,' said The Pedlar. 'He'd eat anything.'

The sergeant folded his arms across his chest and stared at The Pedlar in silence for a little while. Then he shook his head.

'May God forgive you!' he said.

'Why do you say that?' The Pedlar whispered softly.

'You are a very clever man,' said the sergeant. 'There is nothing that the law can do to a man as clever as you, but you'll have to answer for your crime to Almighty God on the Day of Judgement all the same.'

Then he turned to Finnerty and said sharply:

'Come on, Joe. Let's get out of here.'

Finnerty spat on the ground at The Pedlar's feet.

'You terrible man!' he said. 'You wicked dwarf! You'll roast in hell for all eternity in payment for your crime.'

Then he followed the sergeant down along the narrow flagged path that divided the garden.

'Ho! Ho!' The Pedlar cried in triumph as he stared after them. 'Ho! Ho! My lovelies! Isn't it great to hear the mighty of this earth asking for God's help to punish the poor? Isn't it great to see the law of the land crying out to God for help against the weak and the persecuted.'

He broke into a peal of mocking laughter, which he

suddenly cut short.

'Do ye hear me laugh out loud?' he shouted after them. 'No man heard me laugh like this in all my life before. I'm laughing out loud, because I fear neither God nor man. This is the hour of my delight. It is, 'faith. It's the hour of my satisfaction.'

He continued to laugh at intervals, on a shrill high note, while the two men went down the flagged path to the gate and then turned right along the road that led back to Moynihan's sordid cottage.

'Ho! Ho!' he crowed between the peals of laughter. 'I have a lovely satisfaction now for all my terrible shame and pain and sorrow. I can die in peace.'

The metalled heels of his boots now beat a frantic tattoo upon the flagstones and his palsied hands continued to move back and forth over the surface of his blackthorn stick, as if it were a pipe from which they were drawing music.

ALL THINGS COME OF AGE

The baby rabbit was sitting in the sun just by the entrance to his burrow. He was half asleep. His big ears sloped along his back and his sides heaved gently with his breathing. Now and again a slight breeze came up from the stream, raised the brown fur on his side and made silver furrows in it. When the breeze touched him, he sniffed the air and wanted his mother to come and feed him.

He was now big enough to graze for his own food along the fertile bank of the stream, but all his brothers and sisters had been killed by a weasel and for that reason there was still enough milk in his mother's drying udder to feed him. So he had not yet been forced to pluck the short blades of grass with his teeth and chew them. All he did was to come out of his burrow, hop about in the sun, smelling the ground, or sit attentively listening to sound, until something menacing came to his ears and he dived into his burrow for shelter.

At the moment, there was perfect peace by the bank of the stream. The sun was still at its height, although it was long past noon. It shone full on the waterfall, that poured with a wild, sad murmur from a narrow gorge, lined with a thick growth of flowering heather. Like a widespread horse's mane, the water poured from the gorge, thick and brown at its base, where it was coloured by the earth and heather and then, falling, it widened out into a silver sheet. There was a long, deep pool below the fall. Flies skimmed its surface and trout leaped at their gaudy wings. At the near end of the pool, just beneath where the little rabbit dozed, there was a line of boulders thrown across the stream. A wild duck stood on one leg in a hollow between two of the boulders. The duck was asleep, with its bill tucked under one wing.

All was still, except for the drowsy music of the waterfall. Some time ago, when the duck swooped down, quacking, onto the boulders, the little rabbit had taken fright and darted into his burrow. But when he peered out again and watched the duck for a long time, as it fed in the stream, prodding with its beak, he became used to the bird and feared it no more. Now it was asleep and it had become part of the surroundings. There was nothing to be seen of it between the boulders, except its flashing wing feathers and a little of its yellow beak.

Suddenly the duck awoke and withdrew its bill from beneath its wing. It raised its neck and turned its head from side to side, listening. Then it began to bob its head and put both feet on the ground. It moved a little to one side, jerking its head and its tail. Then it quacked. It was a low quack, scarcely audible, but it startled the little rabbit. He became wide awake and moved. At first he laid his ears flat along his back and bent down low to the earth on his stomach. Then he raised himself gradually, thrust forward his ears and listened. He watched the duck.

Now the duck was very excited and began to quack continuously. Shaking its gullet, it paddled about on the boulder, taking tiny steps. The little rabbit became very curious, because he failed to discover the cause of the bird's unrest. There was neither sound nor smell. He raised himself on his haunches, thrust his ears as far forward as he could and let his forelegs drop along his breast. He listened and watched intently. He began to get afraid.

Then the duck uttered a loud quack and swept from the boulders with a great swishing of its wings. It swung in a half circle and then shot upwards into the sky, gathering speed as it rose, until it disappeared over a clump of trees farther down the bank of the stream. The rabbit dropped his forelegs to the ground and gathered himself together to make a dive into his burrow. Yet he did not move. The swoop of the duck and the loud swishing of its wings had so startled him that he could not move. So he remained where he was, crouching.

And then, as he lay crouching, he began to feel afraid. It was the same feeling he experienced a few days previously, when his last remaining brother, having hopped into the clump of briars on the left, had suddenly begun to scream. There was a strange feeling in the air, the nearness of a sinister force, that prevented movement. At that time, however, he had been able to move after a little while and run into his burrow. Now it was different.

The sinister feeling increased. There was absolute silence and there was nothing strange to smell and yet he felt the approach of the sinister force, something unknown and monstrous. In spite of himself, although he wanted awfully to hide from it, he looked in the direction whence he sensed the approach of the enemy. His head shook violently as he glanced towards the boulders that lay across the stream. And then he began to scream. A weasel was crossing the line of boulders.

The baby rabbit had never before seen a weasel, but the long brown body, that moved with awful speed, making no sound, drove him crazy with horror. The weasel paused in the middle of the stream, raised his powerful head and stared at the rabbit, his wicked eyes fixed. And then, keeping his head raised and his eyes on his prey, he glided like a flash to the bank. He disappeared for a fraction of a second behind a stone in his path and then appeared again, standing against the little stone, staring fixedly. Now his powerful head, raised above the long brown barrel of his body, was like the boss of a hammer, poised to strike. The rabbit's screaming became wilder. He was now completely in the brute's power, mesmerized by the staring eyes and by the sinister presence.

The weasel, having mesmerized his prey, was on the point of gliding forward to his meal of blood, when the baby rabbit's mother dashed from the clump of briars on the left, screaming as she ran. She moved in a strange fashion, leaping sideways like a dog trying to sight a hare in a field of corn. It was a grotesque dance, to the accompaniment of wild screams. She passed directly in front of the weasel and circled him twice, threatening him each time with her upraised paws. She drew his eyes from her little one towards herself. When they were fixed on her, she dropped to the ground and began to tremble. She crawled away slowly towards the clump of briars, continuing the while to scream. Then she lay down. The weasel slid from the stone and moved towards her swiftly.

As soon as the weasel's eyes left him, the baby rabbit stopped screaming. Then he began to crawl away upstream. He moved as if his back were hurt. He was almost paralysed and it hurt him terribly to draw his hind legs up under his belly in order to hop forward. But the farther away he went from the weasel, the lesser grew the pain in his joints, until at last it seemed that a weight was lifted from his body and he was able to run, staggering a little, into a great hummock of grass that grew around a gorse bush. He bored a hole through the long, coarse grass with his snout and then lay still in the very middle of it, panting. There he fell asleep.

When he awoke it was late in the evening and the sun had set. He felt very hungry. By now, his paroxysm of fear and the weasel's staring eyes were only a vague memory. He wanted to suck his mother and satisfy his hunger. He backed out of his lair in the grass to look for her. He would find her in the burrow where she always fed him in the evening.

He ran back to the burrow as fast as he could, the little white button of his tail hopping as he ran in the twilight like a ball of cotton carried on the wind. He dived eagerly into the burrow and searched for her. The burrow was empty. He came out again, sat on his haunches and raised his ears, smelling and listening. In the distance, frogs were croaking in a marsh. A curlew called on the wing. A multitude of other birds, about to perch for the night, were warbling. He dropped his forelegs and hopped about, smelling the ground, now and again thrusting forward one ear and then another, listening. All round the mouth of the burrow, among the thrown out earth, that was pebbled with round droppings, he could smell her, but the smell was old and faint. He went farther from the hole, nosing the ground, in search of a fresher scent.

At last he found one, the track on which she had danced before the weasel. He followed it carefully, round and round, until he came to her, over near the clump of briars. She was lying on her side, already stiff in death. Her udder was towards him and he was on the point of thrusting at the nearest teat with his snout, when he drew back slightly, astonished at the unusual odour which her body exuded. He crouched, with his head close into his neck. Then he thrust forward his head once more timidly, and gently smelt her, all along her body. Just beneath her ear the smell was very strange and terrifying. There was a little hole there and the rim of the hole was clotted with dried blood.

As soon as he sniffed the blood, the paroxysm of fear returned. He leaped backwards, sat up on his hind legs, stared at the corpse, squealed and fled to his burrow. He lay in the innermost corner of it, panting.

For a long time he lay there, his head pressed hard against the cold earth. Then again, hunger began to gnaw at his bowels. His hunger gradually became stronger than his fear, driving out the memory of the horrid, clotted blood, around the hole beneath his mother's ear. He forgot his mother. His hunger grew fierce, drowning memory. He crawled out of the burrow.

Night had now fallen and the moon was out, gilding the grassy slope with a fairy light. Several rabbits from neighbouring burrows were grazing in the moonlight. Two little ones, about his own age, were chasing one another. He hopped over to them and began to nibble at the grass.

Dew was now falling on the grass, making it juicy and sweet, just like his mother's milk. When he had eaten his fill, he joined in the dance of the other little rabbits. Now he was no longer afraid and he had completely forgotten his mother. He was one of the herd.

THE FANATIC

Everything in the gloomy tavern, which also served as a general store, was literally covered with dirt. The old wooden counter was dappled like a leopard's hide with dried daubs of porter froth and a labyrinthine pattern of rings left by the bottoms of pint measures. The floor was pocked with holes, some of which were large enough to let a child fall through into the cellar. Rats made a great tumult down below, as they scurried to and fro. The light of day was barely able to penetrate the foul mass of dust and garbage on the window panes. There were thousands of flies roaming about the place, feeding and making love and gambolling at their leisure. The air was laden with a nauseating stench. The sounds of normal healthy life, that came through the open street door from the little country town outside, seemed to be unreal and even plaintive.

Good Lord! It really was like a place invented by Father Mathew, the famous apostle of temperance, while preaching a sermon about the horrors of indulgence in alcohol.

'God save all here,' I said in a loud voice.

Nobody answered and it was hardly reasonable to expect that anybody should; for it seemed that there was nothing alive in the place above ground except flies and the spiders that were trying to catch them in their webs up among the rafters.

'Anybody here?' I called out once more.

'Yes,' said a voice.

I looked to my left and saw a man's face framed between the two posts of the open door that led to the kitchen in the rear. Owing to the poor light, I could see nothing attached to the face. It was like an apparition, that yellow countenance hanging without attachment on the dark air. I got somewhat frightened.

'Good Heavens!' I said to myself, while a tremor of apprehension passed slowly down my spine. 'What place is this? The tavern of the dead? Or has the unaccustomed heat unhinged my reason?'

Then a polite little cough issued from the face and I saw a tall lean man come towards me very slowly behind the counter. He walked with downcast head and he was rubbing the palms of his blue-veined hands together, back and forth continually, in front of his navel. He went past me without glancing in my direction, walking silently on the tips of his toes. After he had passed, he shrugged his narrow drooping shoulders three times in quick succession, a gesture that usually denotes a habital drunkard.

'Thanks be to God,' he said in a gentle low voice, after he had come to a halt in front of the window, 'it's a lovely fine day.'

'Praised be God,' I replied, 'it would be difficult to find fault with it, right enough.'

'It may keep fine like this now for a good spell,' the man said. 'A good spell of it would come in handy.'

'It would,' I agreed. 'It would come in very handy.'

'Oh! Indeed, it would,' he said. 'There's no doubt at all but that a good long spell of it would suit the country down to the ground, in God's holy name.'

Then he clasped his hands behind the small of his

back and let the upper part of his body come slanting gently towards me; exactly like a person on a ship's deck in breezy weather striving to keep his balance against the anarchy of the sea's movement.

'Where was your hurry taking you?' he asked politely.

'It was how I dropped in for a bottle,' I replied.

'Ha! Then,' said he, 'it was a wish for a bottle that brought you.'

'Yes indeed,' said I. 'It was a wish for a bottle of porter.'

He straightened himself suddenly, raised his shoulders and shook his head violently, like a man suffering from cold.

'Upon my soul,' he said, 'you have no reason at all for feeling ashamed of such a wish on a day as boiling hot as this.'

'True enough,' I said, 'it was the heat made me thirsty.'

'Oh! Indeed,' he said with deep feeling, 'it's proud of your thirst you should be on a day like this, instead of feeling the least little bit ashamed.'

Then he looked at me, back over his shoulder.

'Don't be afraid, good man,' he added in a very friendly tone. 'I have a nice fresh bottle for you here, full of porter that is just as sweet and wholesome as the milk of any cow you ever saw in all your natural life. It is, 'faith and no doubt about it.'

He was stiff-necked. He had to turn his whole body right up from his knees before he was able to look me in the face from that position. Good Lord! His eyes were of an extraordinary beauty. They were like a woman's eyes soft and gentle and amorous. It was quite impossible to identify their colour in that dark room. They seemed to be a mixture of brown and grey and green; like the little smooth multi-coloured stones that lie at the bottom of a swiftly-running mountain torrent on whose surface the bright rays of the sun are dancing.

'Come now,' said I. 'Oblige me, in God's name, by handing me that fine bottle. Will you have one yourself, good man?'

He shook his head sadly.

'Thank you, treasure,' he said, 'but I haven't tasted a drop, either good or bad, for the past two years.'

Then he started and began to turn his body ever so slowly, with his head poised in ludicrous immobility on his stiff neck. When he had finally put about, he gave his shoulders a nervous twitch, coughed in his throat and walked towards me on tip-toe. He kept his face turned from me as he went past and his hands were clasped before his navel like a person at prayer. Judging by the movement of his jaw muscles, his lips were framing words. Yet I heard no sound of uttered speech issue from them.

'Oh! Yes,' I said to myself, 'The poor fellow is deranged.'

He picked up a bottle, pulled the cork and filled a glass, which he placed before me on the counter. I gave him a half-crown.

'You are like a man,' he said, while looking for my change in the till, 'that has travelled a fair share of the world.'

'I've been here and there,' I said.

'That's what I thought,' he said. 'You have the cut of a traveller about your wise face.'

'Thank you,' I said.

'You're welcome,' said he.

He approached me once more behind the counter with downcast head. As he was going past, he handed me the change without glancing in my direction. Then he kept moving along slowly on tip-toe, until he reached a tiny wooden cubicle that lay between the end of the counter and the open door that led out into the street. The business accounts of the shop were kept in the cubicle. He thrust his head into it and then stood stock still, with his hands clasped behind his back and his legs spread out wide away behind him: exactly like a frightened sheep hiding its head in a hole and exposing its big tremulous rump to the oncoming danger.

'He's deranged without a doubt,' I said to myself once more.

Then I drank some of the porter and lit a cigarette. In spite of the man's boast, the liquor was sour and almost repulsively tepid. It left a frightful taste on my tongue. Neither of us spoke for some time. The only sound in the shop was the scuffling of the rats down in the cellar. Away out along a country road beyond the town, cart wheels were turning and a man was singing a gay song of love.

'Listen to me,' the tavern-keeper said at last.

'Yes?' I said.

'Were you ever in England?' he said.

'I was,' I said to him. 'Why do you ask?'

He shrugged his shoulders like a toper, pulled his head out of the cubicle and looked at me, turning his body slowly up from his knees, with his head sitting motionless on his stiffneck. His head was like a 'hobby horse' going round in a circle at a fun fair. Now I noticed that it was shaped in a very peculiar fashion. At first, I decided that it was very like the head of a seal, since the skull was no wider than any part of the neck on which it was based. Furthermore, the yellow greasy face was as smooth as a pebble exposed at low tide on a strand. On reflection, however, I came to the conclusion that it was much more like the head of an old stallion, with the neck emerging from the shoulders powerful and broad, tapering as it rose and slanting forward slightly, until it ended in a blunt and naked skull. Except for his eye-brows, his whole countenance was utterly devoid of hair. Even his brows would not provide quite enough material to line a wren's nest.

'It's easy to see,' he muttered in a tone that had suddenly become hostile, 'that you have been in England.'

'Really?' I said.

'Yes,' he said with great emphasis. 'England leaves her mark on everybody that sets foot on her soil.'

'What sort of mark?' I said.

He fixed his glance on the lighted cigarette in my hand.

'The people of England,' he said with maniacal intensity, 'are all pagans, every single one of them. They are, 'faith. Every single one of them is sold to the devil, lock stock and barrel. Sold to the devil in Hell. Red roasting and damnation is their lot in the next world and devil mend them for their greed, that made them sell their souls.'

I looked at him in astonishment and said:

'Are you joking?'

'Joking?' said he. 'Devil a fear of me. I'm in dead earnest. The English are all rotten. That's my final word.'

Thereupon, he thrust his head once more into the cubicle and became absolutely motionless; except for his fingers that were trying to catch one another behind the small of his back. By Jove! The poor fellow's clothes were not worth the ten of clubs. As for dirt! they were really filthy. Neither his shirt nor his jacket possessed a button between them. His twisted shoes were yellow, old with age and neglect. Their tongues were hanging out. They were unlaced. Their leather was scarred and they were down at heel. His bare skin could be seen, here and there, through the holes in his flannel trousers.

'Have you travelled in France?' he said after a while.

I admitted that I knew that country quite well.

'May God forgive you!' he said.

'Why on earth do you say that?' I said.

The queer fellow got excited. He pulled his head out of the cubicle and stared at me in an evil fashion. Now there was bitter hatred in his lovely eyes that were so soft and gentle a short time previously: drowsy with yearning like the eyes of a woman that is dreaming of passionate love. Good Lord! I got afraid that his lunacy had taken charge of his will and that he was becoming possessed by an evil intention.

'The French people are worse than the English,' he said.

'Why do you say that?' I said in a non-committal tone.

'They are lecherous people,' he said. 'There's nothing in that terrible country but dirt and sinful filth. Anybody is in danger of losing his immortal soul that sets foot in it.'

After he had hidden his head once more in the cubicle, I decided to slip away from the place quietly. So I swallowed about half of the porter and then began to make for the door on tip-toe for fear of attracting the strange fellow's attention. However, I did not succeed in effecting my escape. I was just level with the cubicle when he thrust his head suddenly around its side and stared at me. I halted abruptly and returned his stare, with my eyes fixed and my mouth wide open. There we were, the two of us, on either side of the counter, with our faces only a few inches apart, the queer fellow's countenance quivering with hysteria and mine rigid with apprehension. Neither of us spoke for almost a minute.

'Wait,' he whispered at length. 'Wait 'till I tell you.'

'Go ahead,' I said.

'The Americans are the worst of all,' he said. 'They have ruined the whole world with their dirty pictures. They arc spreading adultery and every other kind of sexual filth over the wide world, in the same way that dung is spread to manure a garden.'

'The Americans?' I said.

'Yes,' said he. 'The people of America and it's a terrible thing to admit that some of our own holy race are over there among them.'

'Devil take that for a story,' I said to myself. 'Whether he's mad or sane, that is going a bit too far.'

I put my elbows on the counter and said to him:

'Listen, my good man. You should be ashamed of yourself for insulting in that fashion the whole human race, with the exception of the few that populate this rather insignificant island. Like the fox, you seem unable to smell your own filth. If the first stone could only be cast by a person without sin, it would never be cast.'

I regretted my outburst before I had finished speaking. The poor fellow had begun to shiver from head to foot. The look of hatred had vanished from his eyes, which were soft and dreamy once more. Now, however, it was for pity and forgiveness that they yearned.

'Ah! My dear brother,' he said, 'don't blame me for being foolish and loud-mouthed. I am half dead with loneliness, since, my sister went away two years ago.'

'I understand, brother,' I said. 'In God's name, don't blame me, either for the unmannerly and unkind things that I said.'

'I won't, darling,' he said. 'I know well that it wasn't through wickedness you let out your hasty words into the light of day.'

'Indeed, it was not,' I said. 'A few untidy words very often slip out through a corner of one's mouth, without the mind knowing a thing about them.'

'That's very true, brother,' he said. 'I find myself doing that same, time and again, during the past two years. It's hard to keep the tongue in order when the heart is mad with sorrow. Oh! Darling, I'm telling you that loneliness is a terrible disease.'

'Your sister went away?' I said.

'She did, my pulse,' said he. 'Kate went away to America. She was two years gone away last Feast of St. Brigid. God help us! That was the defenceless blow and don't be talking. It was a death-blow!'

'Yes?' said I. 'There was just the two of you?'

'That was all,' he said, 'since mother died, Lord have mercy on her soul. At that time, Nora had already gone to America and Kate was at a convent school in Dublin. It was to me the place was left and Kate came back home to look after me, since I was in a very delicate state of health. She came back home, right enough, the poor creature and stayed there seventeen years. She did, 'faith. Oh! Indeed, she was as steady a girl as you could meet. As for work! She had no equal as a willing and capable and tidy worker. Ah! Brother, she was a regular saint and no doubt about it. No man ever had a mother kinder that my sister Kate was to me. Look after me? She waited on me hand and foot, as if I were a little naked fledgling in her nest. Oh! Indeed, the two of us were blessed by God and comfortable here in this shop, food and drink and shelter to our name as God ordained for a Christian life, without any need for us to go outside our own door to look for a bit of butter, or a loaf of wheaten bread, or a slice of meat, or a hansel of tea. The good neighbours were going in and out the whole time. The chapel was less than a hundred yards away, down at the end of the street. On a fair day, we'd celebrate a little and drink a sup and sing a couple of songs. Ah! Lord God! That was the lovely life and don't be talking.'

The poor fellow was overcome with emotion and burst into tears.

'Oh! Kate, Kate,' he wailed through his tears, 'you were so gentle and so kind and so holy. Why did you do it? Oh! Why did you?'

Then he turned away from me and went over to the window. His fingers now seemed to be attacking one another savagely behind the small of his back. There was a rattle in his throat. By Jove! I admit that his grief affected me considerably.

'What did she do?' I said gently.

With his back turned towards me, he leaned back from the hips and stared at the roof in the grotesque fashion of a stiff-necked man. His jaws were now bare and his eyes looked savage.

'American pictures!' he said. 'My curse on them!'

'What sort of pictures?' I said. 'Do you mean films?'

'Pictures, I tell you,' he shouted. 'The devil's own pictures, God forgive me.'

He shuddered and continued in a less violent tone.

'They came to our town,' he said, 'about five years ago. A little dark foreigner of a fellow brought them here from Dublin. He used to show them once a week and only young blackguards and corner boys went into the hall, throwing clods of dirt and shouting insults at the foreign lad and breaking the seats. Then the priest spoke from the altar, saying it was only fair to let the foreign fellow earn his living. After that, respectable people began to go to the pictures, especially the women. Soon there were three shows a week and the house full every time. Full of women, young and old. Listen, good man. Women are responsible for all the foreign filth that comes into this holy country. Women! Goats are supposed to be the most inquisitive of all creatures. It is said that if a goat is let as far as the church door, she will end up by eating the altar cloth. Women, though, are even more inquisitive and daring than goats in search of opportunities for committing sin. Women are inclined to sin by nature and a hard discipline is needed to keep them on the right road. Man alive, they are lecherous in the very cradle. Soon after, in any way, they begin to smarten and titivate themselves, getting ready for debauch.'

'Don't blame the poor creatures for their nature,' I said. 'They are just as God created them.'

'Kate began to go to the pictures,' he said, 'and I have it on my conscience that I didn't try to stop her.

What could I say after the parish priest gave the foreign fellow his blessing?'

He turned towards me and he raised his two hands in front of his face, with the fingers turned inward like claws. His eyes shone.

'If I had a hold of that foreign fellow now,' he said viciously, 'I tell you that I'd choke him to death first and then tear the flesh off his bones, strip by strip.'

I moved over gently along the side of the counter until I reached my glass. I swallowed the remainder of the porter, which no longer tasted sour. Upon my soul! I am always timid of lunatics. After I had lit another cigarette, I looked back over my shoulder at the tavern-keeper. He had again thrust his head into the cubicle. His wide-spread legs were far back and his fingers were in frenzied movement behind his back. He was sobbing.

'I had better leave here,' I said to myself. 'It is unmannerly to watch a human soul, when it is laid bare and quivering in the grasp of a great sorrow.'

I was sneaking away on tip-toe to the door, when the heartbroken man gave forth once more in a voice that was hoarse with sobbing. So I came to a halt, lest he might think my going away showed a lack of kindness and sympathy.

'Alas,' he wailed. 'The filthy pictures didn't take long to corrupt her. It was a sort of fright they gave her at first. She used to come home after watching them with terror in her eyes. Then she had nightmares when she went to bed, as if the devil were between sheets with her and he trying to get a strangle-hold on her immortal soul. The damage was done within a month. One day she went to Galway on the bus and when she returned in the evening I hardly knew her. Oh! Lord! She had cropped her hair and all that was left of it on her skull was twisted in the foreign fashion and wet with the sweet oil of lechery. When I began to give her a bit of my mind, it was how she put her fists on her hips and laughed in my face. Making fun of me! Calling me a silly old codger and worse, saving your presence! From that very moment, we took a dislike to each other. There was only argument and complaint between the two of us, that used to be so loving. She kept asking me for money, to buy this and that, from morning to night. She complained about how she had spent the best of her life slaving for me without any reward. True enough, I hadn't given her any money, but it was all between the two of us. All that was earned in the house was put away and neither of us spent any of it. Now, though, she wanted everything changed. She wanted her share and she had to have it. Lord God! May I be forgiven for my sin on the day of judgement! When I should have knocked sparks out of her hide with a stick, it was how I gave way to her in everything. I did, 'faith. I gave her all the money she wanted, for fear she'd go away and leave me alone. I threw it at her without counting it, money that had been hard to earn. Money! She was scattering it like chaff in this direction and in that, just like a mad creature; buying flashy clothes and titivating herself like a whore; painting her finger nails and covering her face with stinking powder; a music-box from England in her bedroom; buying every sort of dainty for the table; sprinkling herself with sweet oil that you could smell from a distance; like the whiff you get in the fall of autumn from a herd of rutting goats. Oh! Lord! The worst of all was when she began to go about in motor cars with the dancing blackguards of the county. Ah! Then, indeed, the sight of her would bring tears from a stone; lovely modest girl that had a saintly mind before America's dirty pictures dragged her down into the ways of sin. At last she took to drink. I'll never forget the night she came home in a motor car and she not able to stand on her feet. When I came down in my shirt to open the door, two men had a hold of her and they barely able to keep her from falling. All three of them, with Kate in the middle, were swaying from side to side in front of the door, singing at the top of their voices. People were sticking their heads out through windows all the way up and down the street. Oh! The terrible shame of it! The three drunkards roared out laughing when they saw me in my shirt. They started to point at my legs and they splitting their sides with laughter. There I was right enough, at three o'clock in the morning, standing in my doorway practically naked and the whole town, you might say, looking at me. Oh! God! That was too much. The whole town seeing me naked! Naked! With only a little shirt that was barely able to ... Oh! God! It was too much. To have her standing there drunk was bad enough, but to have me naked was worse. Naked! You might as well say I was stark naked. I was worse than naked, trying to cover myself with my poor hands. So I cursed her right then and there. I did and I closed the door on her and I shouted out that I never wanted to see her again. Neither did I ever lay eyes on her since. A few days later, a relative came for her clothes. I handed them over, together with half of what money was left in the bank. She went to England then and stayed there a while, until Nora took her out to America. There's where she is now, over in America, thousands of miles away, while I'm here all alone. She might as well be dead for all the good she is to me. Alone! Rotting with loneliness! My heart broken! Oh! Indeed, the devil can have his fun now and plenty of it. He can boast, too, of the fine trick he played on a lovely virgin that was without sin before God. Now it's I myself that has the nightmares and the devil between sheets with me, making terrible fun in the darkness of the night. There isn't anybody even to hear me screech, or to take notice if they heard. Night and day, the devil is whispering in my ear, jeering at me and boasting, saying wicked things that I don't want to understand

and there is a great noise, too, a long way off, with thousands of people threatening me. They have their fists raised and they are shouting a wicked word, over and over again, although what word it is...'

I could understand no more, although he continued to talk in this disjointed fashion for some time further. His words no longer made any sense. His voice, too, gradually became weaker, like a dying breeze, until there was only a pitiful moaning sound coming from his throat. Then he suddenly became silent.

'I must leave here,' I said to myself. 'This is the confessional house of the insane.'

Even so, I was loath to go away without offering a few words of comfort to the stricken man.

'Listen, brother,' I said. 'Why don't you send for her? Perhaps she would come back if you asked her to do so gently, from the fullness of your loving heart.'

He withdrew his head from the cubicle and looked at me in silence for a little while. Now there was dark wisdom in his beautiful eyes and resignation that was much more terrifying than his recent rage.

'Is it Kate?' he said at length.

'Yes,' I said. 'You should write and ask her to come home.'

'She got married six months ago,' he said softly.

Good Lord! I have rarely seen a countenance so forlorn.

'Is that so?' I said.

He went past me without making any reply, walking slowly on tip-toe, on the far side of the counter, with his face turned away and his hands joined in front of his navel, like a person at prayer. After he had gone through the open door leading to the kitchen, he turned and stared at me from out the darkness.

I shuddered again when I saw his yellow countenance hanging, without apparent attachment, on the gloomy air.

Now, however, it was through pity that I shuddered and not at all through fear.

PATSA

OR THE BELLY OF GOLD

There lived in our district an old man called Patsa. He had no doubt been one time young and innocent, but within my memory he had always been aged, wrinkled and a great scoundrel. He embodied within his stinking carcass all the vices and perversions which our ancient community has accumulated through the centuries. For that reason he was greatly feared and respected. He was also a by-word.

He was a tall, lean man, with a solitary yellow tooth in his upper jaw. That tooth was famous and people said when anything was stolen: 'Patsa saw it with his wagging tooth.' For Patsa, being exceedingly cunning, always affected the grin of an idiot, holding his mouth open, showing his naked gums and flicking his tongue against the solitary tooth, which moved hither and thither like a snake's fang.

His eyes were green and small. He had enormous white eyebrows that almost concealed his eyes. His hair had once been white, but it became, later, a dirty yellow colour through lack of moisture. Patsa's body became too mean to feed its own hair, since Patsa was too mean to feed his body. The skin on his face was also yellow and there was no flesh between it and the bone.

His ears were black with dirt and they had as many wrinkles in them as the belly of an aged sow. They were the main cause of the unpleasant odour which Patsa always carried about with him. A chancre had eaten away the top of his nose, leaving a stub which could not possibly be of any use for smelling. The wits of our district said that the nose became diseased through smelling Patsa.

He used to wear a blue tam-o'-shanter cap, a yellow woollen muffler, rawhide shoes and a suit of white frieze. His clothes were generally covered with spots of red ashes and with other unseemly excrements. He made no sound when he walked. He always walked very erect with his hands in his waistcoat pockets. Whenever anybody spoke to him, he stared like a fool for a long time, wagging his tooth. Then, if he had nothing to gain by talking, he said 'Hi' and walked away. If he had anything to gain by talking, he began: 'Well! By the Cross of Christ! May the swine fever devour me if there is a word of a lie in what I am going to say.' He never spoke the truth.

He had no shame in him. Although he had no land and no trade that is considered honourable, he would not fish but begged of the fisherman, who gave unto him in order to drive away his smell. He earned money from strangers and by performing unpleasant jobs. For instance, he had a regular contract for cleaning all the lavatories in the district. In those days there were eight lavatories in the district out of a total of two hundred houses. He also was pleased to accept commissions for burying rotten corpses of animals that had been discovered by the sanitary officer. He was an adept at castration, which he performed at the fixed rate of a penny for a pair of testicles. It gave him such pleasure that he performed the operation free on practically worthless animals like billy goats. Billy goats especially fascinated him. It is recorded that he once was asked to slaughter a particularly evil smelling one by a widow and he offered his services free on the condition that she allowed him to do it with a hatchet. So he hacked the stinking brute and literally cut him to pieces, while a crowd stood about and yelled with joy as the billy goat, tied to a stone by a halter, dodged hither and thither from the blows, with his gore showering about him on the ground every time he shook his head.

He was extremely clever at getting money from strangers. In those days a great number of visitors came to our island. It had just been discovered by the new school of European mysticism and was considered to be the chief reserve of the gods and fairies of the Celtic Twilight. It was by exploiting these mystics that Patsa collected the golden sovereigns which are the subject of this story.

Every time the steamer arrived from the city, Patsa was standing on the pier head, in his dirty white suit, erect, motionless, with his hands in the pockets of his waistcoat, with his yellow muffler and his tam-o'-shanter cap, with his foul ears cocked and his green eyes peering from beneath the rims of his bushy white eyebrows, moving hither and thither like the eyes of a sea hawk, with his mouth open and his tongue fiddling with his solitary, yellow tooth. Nobody escaped him. It was impossible to resist his advances. He had that magnetic quality which is possessed by great whores and by madmen who believe themselves to be gods. He had no fixed method of approach. At times he would dash up and seize a bag and lead the stranger to the hotel and on the way engage himself as guide, porter, storyteller or procureur. With another he might pose as a picturesque fisherman, proud, reluctant, a man to be painted or helped for humanitarian and mystical reasons. With another he became a buffoon and was even seen to dance and pretend to be mad. With another he would rush up and commence with great vehemence to beg, showing false scars on his body like a pariah of the ancient East. He stalked others, appearing before them in lonely places, near ancient fortresses, among the ruins of old churches, leaning against prehistoric pagan stones that are supposed to have occult associations. There, in a hollow voice, he told poets and scholars and dramatists, who are now famous, most of the legends and mystic lore that became current in Ireland and even in Europe during the past generation, relating to the Celtic Twilight.

Patsa, with his foul ears and chancred nose, would descend to any low depths in order to earn a sovereign, or even a sixpenny-bit. It was even said that he tried to sell his own fleas to an English nobleman who collects fleas from all over the world, and made a tour of our district in search of a rare specimen that was said to inhabit the place.

I have laid stress on his cunning in order to give especial point to the manner in which he was finally outwitted by his wife, whom we all thought to be an idiot. Her name was Nuala. She was small and round and plump in spite of old age. She rarely left her own yard. When she saw anybody she always ran into her house, rolling in her gait, like an uneven stone going slowly down a hill. She never had any children. She was noted by the peculiar capacity she had for blurting at will. Indeed, small boys used to call after her: 'Blurt for us, Nuala.'

The unspeakable Patsa even exploited this strange talent of his wife for his own pleasure. He amused himself during the long winter evenings by getting her to kneel on the hearthstone, with her elbows on the ground. Then he would lash her with a dried willow rod, causing her to blurt with great violence. The young blackguards of the neighbourhood were in a habit of crawling up underneath Patsa's window and crouching

there in order to listen to this extraordinary perform-
ance. But one night a young fellow tried to see as well
as hear and brought a torch which he flashed into the
room. Nuala thought it was lightning and went into
a faint, thinking God had punished her for her im-
modesty. From that night she never again allowed her
husband to beat her for the purpose of making her
blurt.

Because of his wife's refusal to satisfy him in this
respect, Patsa redoubled his cruelty in other directions
towards her, and towards all life. He used to crawl up
behind his wife and stick a big needle in her as far as
it would go. As she was short sighted, he used to tie
a rope across the lane through which she went to the
well. He gave her salt instead of sugar for her tea, and he
found great pleasure in exploding a packet of gun-
powder he stole, by throwing into the fire while she was
crouching over it. He gave her no money to buy food
and she had to live on the charity of neighbours.

He himself went about seeking devilment, tying
cords on sheep's thighs, knocking walls, pissing in water
troughs, terrifying people at night by making strange
noises at places that were said to be haunted. He slashed
the canvas of curraghs and set fire to hay and exposed
his person to young women.

But such was the fear in which he was held that
nobody dared interfere with him.

Then suddenly, in his seventy-ninth year, Patsa became
seriously ill and took to his bed. The cause of his
illness was unknown, but was said to result from eating
canned food that had been washed ashore from the
wreck of an American ship. That is plausible enough, as
he became almost paralysed and both his passages closed
up, so that he was given up for lost. Whatever he ate it
made a lump in his stomach and the doctor could do
nothing to relieve him. At last, the doctor told him
that he had only a few hours to live and that he should

send for the priest, confess his sins and get anointed.

Neighbours came in when it was heard that the doctor had told Nuala to fetch the priest. The neighbours were naturally delighted that the good God was at last going to deliver them from such a monster, but they also felt a certain awe at the prospect of losing such a famous one.

The house was an extraordinary sight. From outside it looked like an unused barn, with its stone walls almost naked of mortar, with its thatched roof as hollow as the back of an old stray horse, and with its unpainted door tied by a piece of string. Inside, in the two rooms, there seemed to rest all the smells that Patsa had brought with him from his unsavoury employments. There were great holes in the earthen floor. In a corner there were old potatoes sprouting, with long, unhealthy, white buds sticking up. There was a mound of ashes on the hearth. From the earthen roof and the wooden rafters hung amazing labyrinthine structures made by spiders, in whose meshes lay dead countless enormous flies, beetles and strange insects. The walls were of all colours, caused by rain that dripped through the roof. In the bedroom there was a disreputable bed, on which Patsa was lying, and in a corner a pallet, used by Nuala since her husband got ill. Patsa, lying on his back in bed, with his tam-o'-shanter on his head and his yellow muffler around his neck, as yellow in the face as tanned leather, looked like a devil. Still people came in to console him and to try to prepare him for death as is the custom. For it is said by the founders of the race that even the soul of a dying dog is saved by a pat on the snout and a kind word in the ear.

So they talked to him and told him that God was good and that Jesus Christ was crucified and that the road to heaven was made of angels' wings and that souls were carried up it on a white horse that could twist soogauns with the fastest wind. But they might as well have been harlots whispering in a eunuch's ears for all the notice Patsa took of them.

'Hi!' said Patsa. 'By the Cross of Christ! When sly neighbours come around the bed of death they have the eyes of crows and the only desire they have is to be thieves in the gardens of paradise. But never you fear. My treasure is hidden and I'll be counting it in the company of saints in heaven.'

Then they said to him that he should make his peace now with God and with his wife. In the presence of the priest, they said, it was fitting for him to make provision for the old woman with whatever he had saved, in order to save her withered thighs voyages of beggary from door to door. And they said it must be a queer number of pennies he had saved, since everyone knew that the gentry paid well for having their privies cleaned and whitewashed, and many a stranger had given sovereigns for the stories he told them.

But Patsa answered them and said:

'Hi! Why should I leave her anything, the barren hag? She poisoned me, so I couldn't loose a button for the last eight days.'

The neighbours then went into the kitchen and sat around Nuala, and Nuala wept. The priest came, but Patsa closed his eyes and mouth.

'Make your peace with God and with your wife,' said the priest.

Patsa said nothing. So the priest oiled him and went away. The neighbours also went away. Then Patsa called in his wife.

'Look here,' he said. 'Do what I tell you now, if you don't want me to put my curse on you from my bed of death. Bring me a saucepan full of gruel.'

'I have no meal to make it,' she said, 'Give me the money and I'll fetch it.'

'Go and beg it,' he said. 'Be quick or I'll put a dying

man's curse on you.'

She went and got meal from a neighbour. Then she made the gruel and brought it to him in a saucepan. She stood by the bed to see him take it.

'Leave the room,' he said, 'and close the door after you.'

Nuala left the room and closed the door after her. She was sitting by the kitchen fire for a long time, when at last she heard a terrible groan, then another and then a raucous sound, like a man trying to vomit. She ran into the bedroom.

'Is it choking you are?' she said.

Patsa was speechless. His face was blue. He had his two hands on his belly. The saucepan was on a stool beside the bed. She took it up and looked into it. As she did so the saucepan canted to one side and something rattled against the side amidst the remains of the gruel at the bottom.

'Great God!' she said. 'Did his old yellow tooth fall into the gruel out of his mouth? He must be near dead, sure enough.'

She shuffled out into the kitchen with the saucepan and emptied the remains of the gruel on to a plate. Then she uttered a cry. There were two gold sovereigns among the dregs of the gruel. She ran back into the bedroom and looked at Patsa. Then she saw that he no longer had the yellow muffler around his neck, but that it was lying on the bed. She snatched at it, held it up and then learned what she had been trying to find out for years, poking around the house. It was in the muffler he had hidden his money. It was now ripped and torn in many places and she could see the marks of the little round beds made by the sovereigns.

Then the simple, stupid woman grew as cruel and cunning as a weasel when she realised that Patsa had swallowed his gold in order to take it to the grave with him. He was looking up at her with a queer look of joy in his little green eyes, in spite of his pain. He was enjoying his last perversion with his gut full of gold. He opened his mouth and wagged his yellow tooth in her face.

Then she uttered a wild cry and ran out of the house as fast as her old legs could carry her. She reached a neighbour's house, stood on the floor and cried out, panting:

'Give me, for the sake of God's mother, the oil ye bought for the sick cow, for I must make that old ruffian scutter before the devil snatches him or I'm a beggar woman.'

'Yerrah, what ails ye, woman?' said the neighbour.

'Hand me out that bottle of castor oil,' said Nuala, 'and I'll walk barefoot around the seven temples of the Romans and pray for the souls of your ancestors.'

'Jesus!' said the neighbour. 'He's put a spell on ye. Is it out of yer mind ye are? Sure ye wouldn't give him that dose that is stronger than the dynamite they have for blasting quarries? Let him die in peace.'

'By the fires of hell,' she said. 'He'll die in peace all right, but he'll die with an empty gut, if I have to rip him with my limpet dagger. And I'll make him lose his gold before the sun goes down.'

So then she told the neighbour what Patsa had done, and the neighbour forthwith gave her the pint of castor oil and with it a still stronger concoction made from the juice of limpets and sea-rock weeds. They mixed the two together and went back to Patsa.

When he saw them coming, carrying the horrible mess in a spouty jug, he realised their purpose and made an effort to raise himself and defend his gold. But they laid him flat on the bed, using him roughly and shouting:

'Open your gob now till we empty you, you skinful of lechery.'

'Take care now and make no noise or we'll slice your

instrument with a jagged razor.'

'Aye!' they cried, again and again, and they terrified his dying eyes and his ears with the devilish looks on their faces and the threats that came from their lips.

So he lay still and allowed them to close his nostrils and to prize open his jaws and to pour the jugful down his throat. Then they slapped his belly and gave him a great tumbling and whacking fore and aft, till he began to rumble like a ship's cargo broken loose in a gale. Then they lifted him out of the bed and seated him and he began to void himself.

'Hey! Hey!' said Nuala. 'I knew how to doctor him. Will ye listen to him now? Playing on his drum like a heifer in spring grass. Work away now, ye devil, and I hope yer fundament comes out.'

'Aw! Aw! Aw!' cried Patsa. 'Have pity on me.'

'Devil a pity,' cried Nuala, giving him a great whack between the shoulder blades. 'Deliver every one of them or I'll cut ye open from navel to gullet.'

'Aw!' said Patsa, recovering his speech as he became empty. 'The Jews crucified our Lord Jesus Christ on the cross, but they never jalloped his dying breath.'

'Will ye listen to him blaspheme?' said Nuala. 'By Christ! Ye drove the heart crosswise in me long enough with yer curses, but I don't give a straw for ye now or yer curses.'

Patsa began a long litany of curse. But they, taking no notice of his curses, flung him back on the bed when his labours had ceased. Then they carried off the pot with great joy.

They salvaged the gold and before night came the whole neighbourhood knew of their exploit, for Nuala and her friend promptly got drunk and then returned to the house with a jar of whiskey. Other cronies came and they shook the rafters through the night with their singing of bawdy songs, while Patsa writhed in agony on his bed, listening to them.

A little after midnight, he heard his wife in her drunken gaiety begin an exhibition of her talent for the amusement of her mates. Patsa uttered a loud shriek of rage and died.

THE TEST OF COURAGE

At sundown on a summer evening, Michael O'Hara and Peter Cooke left their village with great secrecy. Crouching behind fences, they made a wide circuit and then ran all the way to a little rock-bound harbour that lay a mile to the southwest. They carried their caps in their hands as they ran and they panted with excitement. They were about to execute a plan of adventure which they had devised for weeks. They were going to take Jimmy the weaver's boat out for a night's bream fishing.

Michael O'Hara was twelve years and four months, five months younger than his comrade. He had very intelligent eyes of a deep-blue colour and his fair hair stood up on end like close-cropped bristles. He looked slender and rather delicate in his blue jersey and grey flannel trousers that only reached half way down his bare shins. Although it was he who had conceived and planned the adventure, just as he planned all the adventures of the two comrades, he now lagged far behind in the race to the port. This was partly due to his inferior speed. It was also due to a nervous reaction against embarking on an expedition that would cause grave anxiety to his parents.

Peter Cooke looked back after reaching the great mound of boulders that lined the head of the harbour. He frowned and halted when he saw his companion far behind. His sturdy body seemed to be too large for his clothes, which were identical with those worn by O'Hara. His hair was black and curly. His face was freckled. He had the heavy jaws and thick nose of a fighter. His small grey eyes, set close together, lacked the intelligence of Michael O'Hara's eyes.

'Hurry on,' he cried in a loud whisper, when Michael came closer, 'What ails you? Are you tired already?'

Michael looked back over his shoulder furtively.

'I thought I saw somebody,' he said in a nervous tone.

'Who?' said Peter. 'Who did you see?'

'Over there,' Michael said.

He pointed towards the north in the direction of the village, which was now half hidden by the intervening land. Only the thatched roofs and the smoking chimneys of the houses were visible. The smoke rose straight up from the chimneys in the still twilight. To the west of the village ran a lane, its low fence standing out against the fading horizon of the sky like a curtain full of irregular holes.

'I think it was my mother I saw coming home from milking the cow along the lane,' Michael said in a voice that was slightly regretful. 'I just saw her head over the fence. but it looked like her shawl. I don't think she saw me, though. Even if she did see me, she wouldn't know who it was.'

'Come on,' Peter said. 'She couldn't see you that far away. We have to hurry or it will be dark before we get the curragh in the water.'

As nimbly as goats, the two boys ran down the sloping mound of granite boulders and along the flat stretch of grey limestone that reached out to the limit of the tide. Then they went into a cave beneath a low cliff that bordered the shore. They brought the gear they had hidden in this cave down to the sea's edge and dropped it at the point where they were to launch the boat.

'Do you think we'll be able to carry her down, Peter?' Michael said, as they ran back across the mound of boulders to fetch the boat.

Peter halted suddenly and looked at his comrade. He was irritated by the nervous tone of Michael's voice.

'Are you getting afraid?' he said roughly.

'Who? Me?' said Michael indignantly.

'If you are,' said Peter, 'say the word and we'll go back home. I don't want to go out with you if you start whinging.'

'Who's whinging?' Michael said. 'I only thought we mightn't be able to carry her down to the rock. Is there any harm in that?'

'Come on,' said Peter, 'and stop talking nonsense. Didn't we get under her four times to see could we raise her? We raised her, didn't we? If we could raise her, we can carry her. Jimmy the weaver can rise under her all by himself and he's an old man. He's such a weak old man, too, that no crew in the village would take him out fishing with them. It would be a shame if the two of us weren't as strong as Jimmy the weaver.'

'I hope he won't put a curse on us,' Michael said as they walked along, 'when he finds out that we took his curragh. He's terrible for cursing when he gets angry. I've seen him go on his two knees and curse when two eggs were stolen from under his goose and she hatching. He pulled up his trousers and cursed on his naked knees.'

'He'd be an ungrateful man,' Peter said, 'if he put a curse on us after all we've done for him during the past week. Four times we drew water from the well for him. We dug potatoes for him in his little garden twice and we gave him a rabbit that we caught. The whole village would throw stones at his house if he put a curse on us after we doing all that for him.'

All the village boats usually rested on the flat ground behind the mound of granite boulders. There was a little wall of loose stones around each boat to protect it from the great south winds that sometimes blew in from the ocean. At present only the weaver's boat remained in its stone pen, lying bottom up within its protecting wall, with stone props under the transoms to keep it from the ground. All the other pens were empty, for it was the height of the bream season and the men were at sea.

'Come on now,' Peter said when they reached the boat. 'Lift up the bow.'

They got on each side of the bow and raised it without difficulty.

'You get under it now and settle yourself,' Peter said.

Michael crouched and got under the boat, with his face towards the stern. He rested his shoulders against the front seat and braced his elbows against the frame. Although they had practiced raising the boat, he now began to tremble lest he might not be able to bear the weight when Peter raised the stern.

'Keep your legs well apart,' Peter said, 'and stand loose same as I told you.'

'I'm ready,' Michael said nervously. 'You go ahead and raise her.'

Peter put on his cap with the peak turned backwards. Then he set himself squarely under the stern of the boat. He gritted his teeth and made his strong back rigid. Then he drew in a deep breath and made a sudden effort. He raised the boat and then spread his legs to distribute the weight. Both boys staggered for a few moments, as they received the full weight of the boat on their shoulders.

'Are you balanced?' Peter said.

'Go ahead,' said Michael.

Peter led the way, advancing slowly with the rhythmic movement of his body which he had copied from his elders. He held his body rigid above the hips, which swayed as he threw his legs forward limply in an outward arc. As each foot touched the ground, he lowered his hips and then raised them again with the shifting of weight to the other foot.

Michael tried to imitate this movement, but he was unable to do it well owing to his nervousness. In practice he had been just as good as Peter. Now, however, the memory of his mother's shawled head kept coming into his mind to disturb him.

'Try to keep in step,' Peter called out, 'and don't grip the frame. Let your shoulders go dead.'

'I'm doing my best,' Michael said, 'but it keeps shifting on my shoulders.'

'That's because you're taking a grip with your hands. Let your shoulders go dead.'

They were both exhausted when they finally laid down the boat on the weed-covered rock by the sea's edge. They had to rest a little while. Then they gently pushed the boat into the water over the smooth carpet of red weed. They had to do this very carefully, because the coracle was just a light frame of thin pine lathes covered with tarred canvas. The least contact with a sliver of stone, or even with a limpet cone, would have put a hole in the canvas. Fortunately the sea was dead calm, and they managed the launching without accident.

'Now, in God's name,' Peter said, imitating a man's voice as he dipped his hand in the seawater and made the Sign of the Cross on his forehead according to ritual, 'I'll go aboard and put her under way. You hand in the gear when I bring her stern to shore.'

He got into the prow seat, unshipped the oars and dipped the glambs in the water before fixing them on the thole pins. Then he manoeuvred the stern of the boat face to the rock. Michael threw aboard the gear, which included a can of half-baited limpets for bait, four lines coiled on small wooden frames, half a loaf of bread rolled up in a piece of cloth, and the anchor rope with a large grarite stone attached. Then he also dipped his right hand in the brine water and made the Sign of the Cross on his forehead.

'In God's name,' he said reverently, as he put one knee on the stern and pushed against the rock with this foot, 'head her out.'

As Peter began to row, Michael took his seat on the after transom and unshipped his oars. He dipped the glambs in the water and put the oars on the thole pins.

'Face land, right hand underneath,' Peter called out just like a grownup captain giving orders to his crew.

'I'm with you,' Michael said. 'Head her out.'

The two boys rowed well, keeping time perfectly. Soon they had cleared the mouth of the little harbour and they were in the open sea. Night was falling, but they could see the dark cluster of village boats beneath a high cliff to the west. They turned east.

'Take a mark now and keep her straight,' Peter said.

Michael brought two points on the dim land to the west into line with the stern and they rowed eastwards until they came abreast of a great pile of rock that had fallen from the cliff. Here they cast anchor. When they had tied the anchor rope to the cross-stick in the bow, the boat swung round and became motionless on the still water.

'Oh! You devil!' Peter said excitedly. 'Out with the lines now and let us fish. Wouldn't it be wonderful if we caught a boat load of bream. We'd be the talk of the whole parish.'

'Maybe we will,' cried Michael, equally excited.

Now he was undisturbed by the memory of his mother's shawled head. Nor was he nervous about his position, out at night on a treacherous ocean in a frail coracle. The wild rapture of adventure had taken full possession of him.

Such was the haste with which they baited and paid out their lines that they almost transfixed their hands with the hooks. Each boy paid out two lines, one on either side of the boat. They had cast anchor right in the midst of a school of bream. Peter was the first to get his lines into water. They had barely sunk when he got a strike on both of them.

'Oh! You devil!' he cried. 'I've got two.'

In his excitement he tried to haul the two lines simultaneously and lost both of the soft-lipped fish. In the meantime, Michael also got a strike on one of his lines. He swallowed his breath and hauled rapidly. A second fish struck while he was hauling the first line. He also became greedy and grabbed the second line, letting the first fish escape. But he landed the second fish.

'Oh! Peter,' he cried, 'we'll fill the boat like you said.'

He put the fish smartly between his knees and pulled the hook from its mouth. He dropped it on the bottom of the boat, where it began to beat a tattoo with its tail.

'Oh! You devil!' Peter cried. 'The sea is full of them.'

He had again thrown his lines into the water and two fish immediately impaled themselves on the hooks. This time he landed both fish, as the lessening of excitement enabled him to use his skill.

'We should have brought more limpets,' Michael said, 'This lot we brought won't be half enough!'

The fish continued to strike. Despite losing a large percentage, they had caught thirty-five before an accident drove the boat away from the school. A light breeze had come up from the land. It hardly made a ripple on the surface of the sea, yet its impact caused the boat to lean away from the restraint of the anchor rope. The rope went taut. Then the anchor stone slipped from the edge of a reef on which it had dropped. Falling into deeper water, it could not find ground. The boat swung round and began to drift straight out to sea, pressed by the gentle breeze.

The two boys, intent on their fishing, did not notice the accident. Soon, however, the fish ceased to strike. They did not follow the boat into deep water. The lines hung idly over the sides.

'They're gone,' Michael said. 'Do you think it's time for us to go home?'

We can't go home yet,' Peter said indignantly. 'We have only thirty-five fish yet. Wait until they begin to strike again when the tide turns. Then you'll see that we'll fill the boat. In any case, we can't go back until the moon rises. It's too dark now to make our way past the reef.'

'It's dark all right,' Michael said in a low voice. 'I can't see land, although it's so near.

Now that the fish had gone away, the vision of his mother's shawled head returned to prick his conscience, and the darkness frightened him as it always did. Yet he dared not insist on trying to make port, lest Peter might think he was a coward.

'They'll start biting again,' Peter continued eagerly. 'You wait and see. We'll fill the boat. Then the moon will be up and it will be lovely rowing into port. Won't they be surprised when they see all the fish we have? They won't say a word to us when we bring home that awful lot of fish.'

Michael shuddered on being reminded of the meeting with his parents after this escapade.

'I'm hungry,' he said. 'Do you think we should eat our bread? No use bringing it back home again.'

'I'm hungry, too,' Peter said. 'Let's eat the bread while we're waiting for the tide to turn.'

They divided the half loaf and began to eat ravenously. When they had finished, Michael felt cold and sleepy.

'We should have brought more clothes to put on

us,' he said. 'The sea gets awful cold at night, doesn't
it?'

'Let's lie up in the bow,' Peter said, 'I feel cold myself.
We'll lie together in the shelter of the bow while we're
waiting for the tide to turn. That way we won't feel the
cold in the shelter of the bow.'

They lay down in the bow side by side. There was
just room enough for their two bodies stretched close
together.

'It's much warmer this way sure enough,' Michael
said sleepily.

'It's just like being in bed,' Peter said. 'Oh! You devil!
When I grow up I'll be a sailor. Then I can sleep every
night out in the middle of the sea.'

They fell asleep almost at once. In their sleep they
put their arms about one another. The moon rose
and its eerie light fell on them, as they lay asleep in
the narrow bow, rocked gently by the boat's movement,
to the soft music of the lapping water. The moonlight
fell on the dark sides of the boat that drifted before the
breeze. It shone on the drifting lines that hung from the
black sides, like the tentacles of an evil monster that
was carrying the sleeping boys out far over the empty
ocean. The dead fish were covered with a phosphor-
escent glow when the boat swayed towards the moon.

Then the moonlight faded and dawn came over the
sea. The sun rose in the east and its rays began to dance
on the black canvas. Michael was the first to awaken.
He uttered a cry of fright when he looked about him
and discovered where he was. The land was now at a
great distance. It was little more that a dot on the far
horizon. He gripped Peter by the head with both hands.

'Wake up, Peter,' he cried. 'Oh! Wake up. Something
terrible has happened.'

Thinking he was at home in bed, Peter tried to push
Michael away and to turn over on his other side.

'It's not time to get up yet,' he muttered.

When he finally was roused and realized what had happened, he was much more frightened than Michael.

'Oh! You devil!' he said. 'We pulled anchor. We're lost.'

There was a look of ignorant panic in his small eyes. Michael bit his lip, in an effort to keep himself from crying out loud. It was a great shock to find that Peter, who had always been the leader of the two comrades and who had never before shown any signs of fear, was now in panic.

'We're not lost,' he said angrily.

'Will you look at where the land is?' cried Peter. 'Will you look?'

Suddenly Michael felt that he no longer wanted to cry. His eyes got a hard and almost cruel expression in them.

'Stand up, will you?' he said sharply. 'Let me pull the rope.'

Peter looked at Michael stupidly and got out of the way. He sat on the forward transom, while Michael hauled in the anchor rope.

'What could we do?' he said. 'We're lost unless they come and find us. We could never row that far with the wind against us.'

'Why don't you give me a hand with the rope and stop whinging?' cried Michael angrily.

Peter was roused by this insult from a boy whom he had until now been able to dominate. He glared at Michael, spat on his hands and jumped to his feet.

'Get out of my way,' he said gruffly. 'Give me a hold of that rope. Look who's talking about whinging.'

With his superior strength, Peter quickly got the rope and anchor stone into the bow. Then the two of them hauled in the lines. They did not trouble to wind them on the frames but left them lying in a tangled heap on the bottom.

'Hurry up,' Peter kept saying. 'We have to hurry out

of here.'

Still roused to anger by Michael's insult, he got out his oars and turned the bow towards the dot of land on the horizon. Michael also got out his oars.

'Left hand on top,' Peter shouted, 'and give it your strength. Stretch to it. Stretch.'

'We better take it easy,' Michael said. 'We have a long way to go.'

'Stretch to it, I tell you,' Peter shouted still more loudly. 'Give it your strength if you have any.'

As soon as he found the oars in his hands, as a means of escape from what he feared, he allowed himself again to go into a panic. He rowed wildly, leaping from the transom with each stroke.

'Why can't you keep time?' Michael shouted at him. 'Keep time with the stern. You'll only kill yourself that way.'

'Row, you devil and stop talking,' cried Peter. 'Give length to your stroke and you'll be able to row with me.'

'But you're supposed to keep with me,' Michael said. 'You're supposed to keep with the stern.'

Suddenly Peter pulled so hard that he fell right back off the transom into the bow. One of the oars jumped off the thole pin as he fell backwards. It dropped over the side of the boat and began to drift astern. Michael turned the boat and picked up the oar.

'Don't do that again,' he said as he gave the oar to Peter. 'Listen to what I tell you and row quietly.'

Peter looked in astonishment at the cruel eyes of his comrade. He was now completely dominated by them.

'It's no use, Michael,' he said dejectedly. 'You see the land is as far away as ever. It's no use trying to row.'

'We'll make headway if we row quietly,' Michael said. 'Come on now. Keep time with the stern.'

Now that he had surrendered to the will of his comrade, Peter rowed obediently in time with the stern oars. The boat began to make good way.

'That's better,' Michael said, when they had been rowing a little while. 'They'll soon be out looking for us. All we have to do is keep rowing.'

'And where would they be looking for us?' said Peter. 'Sure nobody saw us leave the port.'

'They'll see the boat is gone,' Michael said. 'Why can't you have sense? I bet they're out looking for us now. All we have to do is to keep rowing quietly.'

'And how would they see us?' Peter said after a pause. 'We can hardly see the land from here, even though it's so big. How could they see this curragh from the land and it no bigger than a thimble on the water?'

Michael suddenly raised his voice and said angrily:

'Is it how you want us to lie down and let her drift away until we die of hunger and thirst? Stop talking and row quietly. You'll only tire yourself out with your talk.'

'Don't you be shouting at me, Michael O'Hara,' Peter cried. 'You better watch out for yourself. Is it how you think I'm afraid of you?'

They rowed in silence after that for more than two hours. The boat made good way and the land became much more distinct on the horizon. It kept rising up from the ocean and assuming its normal shape. Then Peter dropped his oars and let his head hang forward on his chest. Michael went forward to him.

'I'm thirsty.' Peter said. 'I'm dying with the thirst. Is there any sign of anybody coming?'

'There is no sign yet, Peter,' Michael said gently. 'We have to have courage, though. They'll come all right. Let you lie down in the bow for a while. I'll put your jersey over your face to keep the sun from touching you. That way you won't feel the thirst so much. I heard my father say so.'

He had to help Peter into the bow, as the older boy was completely helpless with exhaustion. He pulled off Peter's jersey and put it over his face.

'Lie there for a while.' he said, 'and I'll keep her from drifting. Then you can spell me."

He returned to his seat and continued to row. He suffered terribly from thirst. He was also beginning to feel the first pangs of sea-hunger. Yet he experienced an exaltation that made him impervious to this torture. Ever since his imagination had begun to develop, he had been plagued by the fear that he would not be able to meet danger with courage. Even though he deliberately sought out little dangers and tested himself against them without flinching, he continued to believe that the nervousness he felt on these occasions was a sign of cowardice and that he would fail when the big test came.

Now that the big test had come, he experienced the first dark rapture of manhood instead of fear. His blue eyes were no longer soft and dreamy. They had a look of sombre cruelty in them, the calm arrogance of the fighting male. His mind was at peace, because he was now free from the enemy that had lurked within him. Even the pain in his bowels and in his parched throat only served to excite the triumphant will of his awakening manhood. When his tired muscles could hardly clutch the oars within his blistered palms, he still continued to row mechanically.

In the afternoon, when the village boats finally came to the rescue, Michael was still sitting on his transom, trying to row feebly. By then he was so exhausted that he did not hear the approach of the boats until a man shouted from the nearest one of them. Hearing the shout, he fell from his seat in a faint.

When he recovered consciousness, he was in the bow of his father's boat. His father was holding a bottle of water to his lips. He looked up into his father's rugged face and smiled when he saw there was no anger in it. On the contrary, he had never before seen such tenderness in his father's stern eyes.

'Was it how you dragged anchor?' his father said.

Although his upper lip was twitching with emotion, he spoke in a casual tone, as to a comrade.

'It could happen to the best of men,' the father continued thoughtfully after Michael had nodded his head. 'There's no harm done though, thank God.'

He put some clothes under the boy's head, caressed him roughly and told him to go to sleep. Michael closed his eyes. In another boat, Peter's father was shouting in an angry tone.

Michael opened his eyes again when his father and the other men in the boat had begun to row. He looked at the muscular back of his father, who was rowing in the bow seat. A wave of ardent love for his father swept through his blood, making him feel tender and weak. Tears began to stream from his eyes, but they were tears of joy because his father had looked at him with tenderness and spoken to him as to a comrade.

WILD STALLIONS

As he stood guard over his grazing herd, on a hillock near the northern wall of his lofty mountain glen, the golden stallion's mane and tail looked almost white in the radiant light of dawn. At the centre of his forehead, a small star shone like a jewel.

The rigid thickness of his lower neck, together with the many scars of former battles on his glossy hide, showed he had passed his prime. Even so, the erect and noble stance of his muscular and compact body also proved he still possessed great power and energy and dauntless courage.

Staring intently towards the south, his small ears pricked and his nostrils opened wide, he was trying in vain to discover the exact nature of a menacing scent with which the light and intermittent breeze was charged.

Down there, his domain ended in a steep and narrow pass that wound through precipitous cliffs to the vast plains of the lowland desert. The pale shroud of night, like a drawn curtain, still covered the wide and over-arching mouth of the ravine, so that his keen sight was baulked of its full use at that point; while the faint and vacillating gusts of wind, laden so heavily with many other scents in their aimless wandering, left him ignorant of their message in spite of his skill.

Now and again, the agony of suspense made a tremor run along his spine and he pawed the earth in impotent rage.

Then he saw the vague figure of a horse suddenly appear for a brief moment, like a phantom, through the drifting mist. Uttering a shrill cry of warning to his herd, he sprang into a gallop at once and ran the whole length of the glen at top speed. The stranger had vanished when he reached the mouth of the pass. On the ground, however, he found material proof of the furtive creature's recent presence.

The tumbling stream that flowed along the western side of the glen, through a shallow bed of smooth red stones, spread out into a wide and foam-embroidered pool before going underground within the dark mouth of the ravine. A few feet from its bank, where the fine sand had been freshly-trodden by the hooves of a drinking horse, smoke rose in a slender twisting column from a round patch of wet grass and the immediate air overhead was rank.

As soon as he caught sight of the tell-tale evidence, the golden stallion halted abruptly and laid back his ears. With his jaws bared, shuddering from head to foot, he stared at the twisting column of smoke and sniffed the fetid air for several moments. Then he stretched out his neck and began to advance slowly; putting each foot forward with great care.

He was about to lower his head, to make a close inspection of the new made stale, when a shrill and arrogant neigh put an end to all uncertainty about its origin. Turning aside swiftly, his tail arched, he got set to attack the sly outcast, come to fight for possession of his mares.

The mature cunning of his years made him reject

the hot impulse of his outraged blood to seek battle at once; knowing it would be madness to enter the gloomy depths of the ravine; where the sides of the sheer cliffs were hollowed; where his enemy could hide in one of the clefts and watch him go charging past and leap from behind unawares to deliver a death-blow. For that reason, he galloped out into the open glen a little way and then neighed defiantly three times; rising on his hind legs to paw the air and lashing both flanks with his tail.

The invading enemy was equally cunning. He answered with a mocking cry and remained hidden.

The golden stallion continued to challenge without avail, prancing back and forth before the mouth of the ravine, until he noticed that his herd was running in panic through the upper part of the glen. It took him a long time to subdue and pen the frightened creatures in a large cavern near the centre of the northern wall. Leaving them in charge of the oldest colt, a stalwart fellow that was getting ready to become a sire, he galloped back to his post.

After goading the unseen and silent enemy until noon, he turned the herd out to graze on the upland. Then he selected three of his unbroached fillies and drove them down to the pass; hoping the lustful exaltation inspired by their presence would overcome the sly invader's guile and persuade him to give immediate battle. In order to enrich the lure, he himself even mimed the tumult and ecstasy of mating with all the skill of his veteran experience.

Once again, the furtive outcast refused to be flushed from cover and showed no sign of life.

When night fell, the golden stallion enclosed his herd and guarded the cavern entrance. By then, he had begun to feel the strain of his prolonged and fruitless struggle. The darkness irked him terribly. Ignorance of the enemy's position and design kept pressing on his taut nerves like a vice. He snorted and leaped clean into the air at every sound; the scream of an attacked bird; the wail of coyote, the tinkling fall of a dislodged pebble along the face of a cliff.

In spite of his hunger, he never once stooped to pluck a few blades of grass.

Next day, he changed his tactics and pretended to ignore the hidden presence of his enemy. Even so, the herd gave him very little chance to rest; or to renew his strength by grazing. Again and again, the older mares led sorties into the rich pastures at the centre of the glen. He had to punish them severely before they consented to go north; where the stony ground was almost barren.

Later, he had to contend with a peculiar form of panic that was still more exhausting to control. Rushing together suddenly in a compact mass, the new-born foals at the centre, the mares lowered their heads and whinnied on a plaintive note. He had to charge into their midst repeatedly, bite their necks and lash out at the most obstinate with his hooves. On those occasions, the novice became hostile and even rebellious.

During the afternoon, vultures began to settle on the brows of the surrounding cliffs. Up there, too, wolves were trotting back and forth restlessly in small groups; together with a pair of mountain lions. Eagles soared high in the firmament. They all watched the glen and the mouth of the ravine; looking down with intense and expectant interest.

At midnight, the waiting enemy broke silence. In a voice that was tender and tremulous, he addressed a serenade to the enclosed mares. Each prolonged neigh, that echoed and re-echoed through the high-walled glen, made known his loneliness, his virgin power and his fierce will to beget his kind in majesty. Now and again, however, he suddenly changed his tone and put all the male force of his being into a triumphant shriek of passion.

The watching beasts and birds of prey joined their forlorn cries from on high to his vainglorious pleading, as if they longed to share in the wanton ecstasy of which he sang.

Lunging to and fro on guard, the golden stallion answered each call of his seducing enemy in a voice that hunger and anxiety had hoarsened. His hollow flanks were dark with the cold sweat of incipient panic. Sudden pain struck deep into his weary heart from time to time, as he saw the red eyes of the watching beasts and birds of prey all round him in the darkness, like sombre lamps of death hung out in vigil for the morrow's battle.

Shortly after dawn, the proud invader strode out through the curtain of drifting mist; his head erect and his limber body swaying in the buoyant rhythm of arrogant youth. Although his immature bones were somewhat light for the violent stress of close combat, the resilience of his graceful carriage showed he was very fast and supple in manoeuvre. His nimble hooves seemed merely to caress the ground as he came delicately forward; looking gay and handsome and resplendent; the brilliant sunlight dancing on his grey hide dappled with small white spots.

On reaching the centre of the glen, he neighed in his throat and bowed his head three times in quick succession; as if saluting his opponent with courteous and proper ceremony. Then he arched his tail and began to climb the gentle slope at a canter; lifting his fore legs high and swinging his neck from side to side in order to prepare his muscles for the moment of onset.

Turning and turning in his tracks over the torn ground, the golden stallion waited to give battle with savage joy. Although his flanks were still moist with the foaming sweat of panic, the imminence of combat had made his heart defiant. His blood-shot eyes were fixed in a stare and his nostrils shivered like wind-blown leaves. His herd and his hunger and the wasteful torture of suspense were all forgotten. The glorious intoxication of the lust to kill had taken full possession of his being.

When the enemy was half way up the slope, the two stallions shrieked in unison and charged. The thud of their hooves, racing over hard earth, was almost drowned by the violent outrush of their breath. At a distance of about one hundred yards, they both neighed once more on a shrill note and canted their arched necks stiffly to the right.

Just before they met, the invader turned aside and swung his hind legs upward in an arc. The golden stallion's head just missed being crushed by the flying hooves as he veered instinctively to the left and struck the exposed flank a heavy glancing blow with his chest. The unbalanced enemy was tossed and thrown to earth on his back with stunning force. Even so he did not lose his wits. After rolling down the slope three times, he rose and defended himself with great skill against the furious efforts of the golden stallion to break through and deliver a death-blow.

At times, the supple grey leaped high into the air above his own ground. Twisting and turning while aloft, like a cat at play, he snapped his bare jaws and kicked in all directions. Then again, he plunged hither and thither; his head low between his fore legs; bending and stretching his back; swaying his crupper as it rose and fell in constant movement;

The golden stallion was gored several times, in his neck and chest, before they suddenly broke contact and galloped towards the south at half pace.

They ran abreast, tails at rest, their heads turning nonchalantly from side to side; like comrades pleasantly at exercise. Near the pass, they turned outwards in a wide arc and went north, skirting both sides of the glen, without apparent interest in each other until coming into line with their terrain. Then, they shrieked and charged in unison.

At the moment of contact both swerved and ran southwards in close combat; making long thin figures of eight as they barged and fell away to barge once more in fierce collision. They swung their hind legs at the opponent's groin during each outward lunge and snapped at his jugular vein when their shoulders met.

Half way down the glen, they became exhausted and drew apart to get ready for the final onset.

As he trotted in a slow circle, the grey invader kept rising to paw the air and shriek defiance. Only a few minutes had passed since he strode out from the ravine in arrogant splendour and conceit; lusting to squander his rich purse of virgin seed on the spoils of victory. Yet his shining body had already shrunk and grown old in the torment of battle. Blood poured from his nostrils. His staring eyes were crazed with pain. Each time his darkened flanks heaved with the effort to draw breath, a pale cloud of smoke issued from his scarred hide and covered him from head to foot.

The golden stallion had fared still worse. His legs were so numb he could barely stand erect and firm. His great bulk was racked and torn by wounds from end to end. Several of his ribs were broken. Even the sack of his genitals had been sorely touched by a hoof. A rivulet of blood flowed from his slack underlip. One eye was closed and the other's sight had grown so dim that he could only see the prancing enemy as a vague and formless shape.

By then, the beasts and birds of prey had all come down from the cliffs to be on hand for the kill.

The vultures were the first to arrive, alighting in small groups around the scene of combat. Some waddled to and fro casually on their bandy legs. Others stared solemnly at the combatants, their dark wings raised like screens about the obscene red skin of their bald heads. Creeping northwards from the pass in four separate bands, the wolves lay down flat at short intervals to sniff the shed blood and whine hungrily. They were followed by three mountain lions that yawned and stretched their backs; as if bored by the long wait.

On seeing all those enemies approach, the novice hastily prepared to carry off the unbroached fillies and the younger mares that had no foals at foot. After driving the unwanted dams to the rear with their helpless young, he herded his chosen consorts at the cavern's mouth in close order of flight. Then he strove to bind them to his person with caresses and passionate cries; while waiting for the proper moment to break out of the glen.

The final onset began without ceremony. Neighing hoarsely in his throat, the invader cantered forward slowly with his head bowed. The golden stallion stood his ground on widespread legs, mustering the last remnants of his strength, until the enemy swerved at close quarters to deliver a broadside. Then he rose and brought his forelegs down with great force. Struck above the kidneys, the grey uttered a shrill cry and fell. While rolling away, a second blow on the spine made him groan and shudder from head to tail. With his glazed eyes wide open, he turned over on his back, swung his neck from side to side and snapped his jaws without known purpose in the urgent agony of death.

When the golden stallion tried to rise once more and strike, his legs were no longer able to bear his weight. He staggered forward; bending at the knees. While he plunged hither and thither, in an effort to regain his balance, the enemy's teeth closed on his right hind leg above the fetlock. Then he, too, shrieked and fell sideways over the belly of his prostrate enemy who made a gurgling sound in his throat and let his jaws hang open.

Then, the novice broke from the cavern with his compact troops and galloped towards the south at full speed. Neighing constantly on a fierce note, they passed beneath a dark cloud of vultures flying in haste to the fallen combatants. A few of the foremost wolves leaped at their flanks and got gored; others slunk aside in awe of their discipline and power. Long after they had entered the ravine and disappeared, the thunder of their hooves continued to resound among the over-arching cliffs.

Roused by the squawking birds of prey, swarming over the outstretched neck of his enemy, the golden stallion rose and hobbled away on three legs. As soon as he had gone, the whole carcass of the grey invader got covered by a sombre mound of flapping wings. Here and there, obscene red heads broke through the undulating mass; like buds thrusting forth into the light from polluted earth.

Whinnying on a tremulous note, the abandoned mares and foals ran to their crippled sire. Made valiant by his presence, they kept the charging wolves at bay for a little while.

Then two of the mountain lions broke through the circle and brought him down.

THE MERMAID

In the village of Liscarra there lived a young man who was famous for his strength and beauty. From end to end of the coast his name was like sweet honey on the lips of the people. To strength and comeliness, the two most-coveted virtues in our Western land, Nature had added countless others no less desirable. So that it seemed a young god had come to live among us. Instead of jealousy, it was a godly pride that he aroused in others, young and old; pride that such a one had been born of their race.

In spring time, when young horses were being broken on the long strand by the seashore, it was Michael McNamara who was chosen to tame the wildest, and no man ever saw him thrown. It was a great joy to hear him shout the wild calls of the horseman as he raced by the sea's edge, with one hand grasping the mane, the other swinging the long halter about his golden head, while the sunlight glittered on the horse's naked hide and the unshod hooves splashed through the foaming wash of the waves. He could throw an ox single-handed with one twist of the beast's horns. People vied with one another to have him in the prow of their boat at sea; both for his skill as an oarsman and because it seemed to them that the cruel sea would not dare to drown one who was the favourite of God.

At church on Sundays young women blushed at their prayers, feeling him in the same house with them.

Most wonderful of all his gifts was the subtle genius of his hands. He could make a boat with wood and a house with stone and a basket with willow rods. Indeed, he seemed to be master of all crafts by the grace of Nature, so that music, which is a special gift among us, mostly always reserved for the blind and the weak as compensation, was also his, in its fullest sweetness. No blackbird at sunset ever sang with finer melody than he, and with a fiddle his fingers wove those wild sweet tunes that have been handed down through many generations from our ancient poets, who, by their divine witchcraft, so it's said, learned the piping of the birds.

Everything prospered with him, yet he coveted nothing, neither wealth nor position; neither did he put his talents to the base purpose of gain, as is customary with the avaricious, but he did everything free, for the love of his neighbours. He lived simply like others less gifted and less fortunate, tilling his land and fishing in the sea and carousing with the young men at festival times.

He was twenty-six when his mother died. She had no other children, and his father had died three months after Michael was born. Such was the young man's innocence that he never shed a tear on his mother's death, and he followed her to her grave smiling. He did not understand the meaning of sorrow. When his relatives rebuked him for his levity, he told them that it would be foolish to mourn for one who had gone to share eternal happiness with the saints.

After his mother's death he lived alone in his house for two years without thought of marriage, although the finest women in the district were offered to his relatives, as is the custom. When the parish priest rebuked him for his celibacy, saying it would lead him into debauchery and sin, he said that a man who had to be muzzled by a wife as a protection against debauchery was not worthy of the joy of innocence. After that people began the treat him with priestly respect.

Then at the great horse fair of Ballintubber, there was a man of the family of Conroy, who had come down from the mountains with three horses for sale. They were three beauties, bred from the same mother, and people remarked that a great sorrow or a greater want must have forced their owner to put himself in the way of parting with them. For among Western people a beautiful horse has no price. McNamara got into conversation with this man, while the jobbers were examining the animals and shouting out their faults to the rage of their owner, who knew them to be without blemish.

'This is a terrible day,' he said, 'for my father's son, to be selling my last three horses to strangers of foul mouths and I that can remember the day when there was a score of horses of that breed grazing free on the mountain. But I have a daughter that has to be portioned.'

'Well!' said McNamara. 'If your daughter is as beautiful as your horses I'll take her without any portion.'

'And who may you be?' said Conroy.

'I am Michael McNamara of Liscarra. I am well known among my people.'

With that, the stranger shook McNamara by the hand and they retired with their relatives to a tavern, where they drank one another's health, and that evening they all set out to the mountains to see the young woman. When McNamara saw her his innocence and his happiness left him, for she was more beautiful than he.

He took her by the hand, and he said to her:—

'It's a poor boast for the young men of your country to say that they let your father drive his horses to the fair to portion you, for you are more beautiful than the morning sun. But you are as cruel as the March wind. I brought your father's horses back from the fair of Ballintubber to his door unsold, and you have numbed my heart in return for this kindness. Now you'll have to marry me, before you add to your cruelty by killing me with desire for you.'

Indeed, desire came upon him with the frenzy of a wild hurricane that comes rushing on a summer day out of the ocean in the west, laying waste all before it. And she was worthy of such love.

When the foam bubbles are flying in the wind above the cliff-tops on an April day and the gay sun, shining through the rain, is mirrored in their watery globes, they are more beautiful than rare pearls. Such were this girl's eyes, jewels of maddening beauty. Her raven hair was haloed by the shimmering light that the full moon casts upon the sea, within dark bays, where rock birds nod upon their ledge, hushed by the enchantment of the night. She was dressed simply, as was fitting for one so beautiful; for the richest clothes would but defile her body, that was made to be adored in its white innocence by wondering eyes, naked, like the pretty flowers that open wide their petals to the bee.

But, alas! Rank weeds that sprout in March still flourish in their ugliness when the autumn winds are singing of the winter's snow, while the most tender blossoms lose their fragrance from dawn to sunset of one summer day. So with this girl. Her beauty was too perfect to endure. Already the red flush of death was on her cheeks.

She returned his love, and on the feast of Saint Martin that autumn Margaret Conroy became the wife of Michael McNamara in the parish church of

Liscarra. People shed tears in the church, and a crowd like an army followed them home to the wedding.

They lived together in an ecstasy of happiness for a month. During the rare moments when they were not in one another's arms, McNamara went about like one entranced, overpowered by the amazing passion that had come to him. And she, giving herself with the frenzy of the doomed, burned in the heat of his caresses until, to his horror, one morning he awoke beside her to find the pallor of death on her lips.

She was dead within a week. Wise old women that followed her corpse to the grave said that a convent was the proper place for such frail beauty; that it could only live wedded to the gentle Christ. Others, who still believed in the ancient sorceries, said that the God Crom had taken her for his bride.

McNamara lost his reason. He refused to believe that she was dead and walked behind the coffin in a stupor, but when he saw them lower the coffin into the grave and shovel earth upon it, he uttered a wild shriek and threw himself into the pit. They dragged him out and took him away, still shrieking, but he broke from their arms and ran wild into the country, tearing his hair, wailing aloud, cursing God, his mother and the day he was born. He gashed his face with thorns and tore off his clothes. At last they caught him and brought him home. The people came to comfort him.

When the first outburst of his sorrow had exhausted itself and his reason returned, he said to the people who had come to comfort him:—

'Why do ye talk to me about the love of God, who is so cunning in His cruelty? Did I not see her put down into the earth among the worms? Why do ye tell me that time will cure the sorrow of my heart, when I know that from now to my last breath I can only have a curse for the sun that rises with the dawn and for the birds that sing with the fall of night? Go away from me all of you and leave me here alone in this house where I can still feel the sweetness of her breath.'

He who had been as beautiful and meek and happy as a god in his innocence was now uncouth in his sorrow. The people fled from his scowling face. He sat all day by his empty hearth, in silence with his grief. At dead of night, when the terrible moon came shining through the windows of his house, he softened into tears and went barefooted to the bed where he had lain with her. He kissed the pillow which her head had touched, whispering her name. Then she appeared near to him and he forgot the grave in which they had buried her. So he slept. But next morning, when he awoke and found an empty place where she had lain beside him, his anguish returned with greater force. He passed the day, sitting in silence by his cold hearth.

Towards evening the first storm of winter gathered in the east and the thunder of the sea reached the village loudly. Then he heard her calling him. He went out of the house and saw the sea birds in the sky, going inland from the sea that was rising. The sky was magnificent with purple and black clouds and the roar of thunder and the brilliant lightning flashes incited him to a frenzy of delirium, for he thought this tumult was the voice of God, repenting for having stolen his beloved.

He went from the village to the seashore. There, in a rockbound cove, on a sandy place, the village boats were lain. He took one of them, with oars, and pushed it into the tide. And he rowed out to sea. Soon the frail craft was tossing on great breakers and carried westwards by the wind, beneath the towering cliffs.

Then he heard her voice, above the roaring of the wind, singing to him, and he cried out:—

'Margaret, my loved one, where are you? I am coming.'

Then his sorrow vanished and his heart grew light and his eyes shone in ecstasy and he rowed towards the cliffs, carried by the great waves, that rolled like mountains to the concave walls of stone. Now he heard her voice clearly, singing to him, quite near, a song of enchanting sweetness. He dropped his oars, stood up in the boat, and turned towards the cliff, whence her voice had come to him.

As the wave carried his boat at headlong speed towards the cliff, he saw her, with her arms stretched out, beckoning to him. Her raven hair was crowned with glittering sea-foam and it streamed down her naked white shoulders. She wore a belt of sea-gems. Her feet were winged. She stood at the door of a cave that had opened in the cliff's face, and beyond her, within the cave, he saw a palace of dazzling beauty.

Then the wave struck the cliff, sending a column of hissing brine high into the firmament, and at the same instant his arms closed about her wraith and he swooned into an ecstasy of eternal love.

THE ENCHANTED WATER

Nearly every bit of land around this lake, the old fisherman said, is named after some kind of bird. The broad flat crag where we're sitting is called 'The Sea Gull's Perch'. It was given that name because sea gulls come down here from the high southern cliffs when bad weather makes it impossible for them to get any food from the raging sea.

Sea gulls are very clever birds. They always know before hand when a storm is coming. If you look up from the village on a fine summer day like this and you see a crowd of them walking about on these smooth grey flags, or flying low over the lake out there in front, with their legs hanging and their eyes searching the water for a morsel of food, then you may be sure that the weather is going to break before many hours have passed.

That low cliff that rises sheer above the far side of the lake, with ivy growing all along its face, is called 'The Heron's Rock'. There are four herons standing on top of it now, with their wings raised up about their heads, like long-legged fellows trying to protect the backs of their necks from a shower of rain. They are even smarter than the sea gulls, although it would be hard to say where they keep their brains, and their heads so small compared to the rest of them. You never see them except when a spell of dry weather has made the lake water low like it is now. Then they can stand on the bottom and fish for eels with their long necks. It really is a mystery to me how they know the right time to come, for I swear that I never in all my life have known them to arrive a day too soon or too late.

The lake itself has two names. It's officially known as 'The Black Lake', but the local people call it 'The Enchanted Water' among themselves. It looks lovely and gay now in the sunlight, with swans swimming along its smooth white surface and curlews standing in sleep on the little yellow patches that have gone bare and water hens chasing one another among the reeds. You would agree, though, that it was given two fitting names, if you come here in winter, when the surrounding cliffs and its own deep water are black with rain and a sound like the whispering of sad women comes from the reeds that are shaken by the fierce wind.

In the old days, people believed that it was haunted by a wicked spirit. Indeed, some of them believe that still. It would be hard to find a person in our village brave enough to come here alone on a dark windy night. The young women carry away some of its water in big sea shells and use it for charms. They say that no woman ever dies barren or in childbirth if she says certain prayers and then drinks the lake water out of a sea shell. It is also supposed to be very good for cattle, the water of this lake. People drive their beasts here from all over the countryside, especially in spring, to drink their fill. It's claimed that no horse is as swift as a horse that drinks from 'The Enchanted Water'. Oh, people sometimes say more than the truth; but there is a grain of truth is everything that's handed down from ancient times.

It is also handed down that a saint lived here alone,
a very long time ago. They say he was so grateful to
the birds for keeping him company that he blessed
them and put his curse forever on anybody that would
do them harm. For that reason, the place has remained
a sanctuary down to the present day for nearly every
kind of lake bird in creation. Even the most daring
and mischievous boy in our village would rather cut
off his right hand than throw a stone at one of the
birds that live here, or rob their nests. The birds themselves know they are safe. They are not the least afraid
of people. Curlews are the most suspicious and wary
creatures in existence, as a general rule. Yet there are
two of them standing on that black rock down below
us, with their heads under their wings, feeling just as
secure as children being rocked in a cradle.

The saint is also supposed to have divided up all
the ground along the edge among the different tribes
of birds, in order to keep them from fighting one another. They say it was he named each little spot after
the kind of bird that he let build its nest there and take
its ease in the sun. That part of the story can't be
entirely true, because I myself was responsible for
giving its name to 'The Wild Drake Cave' about thirty
years ago. Previous to that time, it had no name at all
to my certain knowledge.

You can see the cave's entrance from here, over on
the far side of the lake, a short distance to the right of
the herons. You can't miss it. It's like a round black
windows set in the smooth grey face of the cliff. There
is a big patch of white moss almost directly overhead
and trout are jumping in the shadows down below.
The hole is a good few yards from the water's edge
now, but when the lake is full a swimmer could almost
reach it with his upraised hand. Even so, the smallest
child couldn't pass his body through it and the smooth-

ness of the surrounding cliffs keeps out creatures like rats and weasels. Only birds can enter. It's an ideal nesting place.

As I said before it was nearly thirty years ago that I gave its name to that cave. This is how it happened. One morning in late spring, I brought my cow down to the low shore, far over there to the right, where you see three black horses standing knee-deep in the water. While my cow was having her drink, I noticed a duckling that was trying to hide itself among the muddy grey stones by the lake's edge. It made hardly any effort to escape as I approached. When I picked it up and laid it on my palm, it just gave one little squeak and that was all. It was half dead with cold and hunger; a poor little defenceless thing still wearing the down of infancy. As I could find no trace of its parents anywhere, I came to the conclusion that it was either deserted or lost. So I put it inside my shirt and took it home with me.

As luck would have it, my wife was raising a clutch of ducklings at the time. Since she couldn't find a brooding duck, it was a hen that hatched out the eggs for her. Then the hen deserted the ducklings as soon as they were born. I suppose the foolish creature got frightened when she saw the strange cut of them and took to her heels. In any case, my wife had to put them on a litter of straw in a wooden box near the kitchen fire and tend them herself. They were not much older than the wild creature I had found.

'In God's name,' I said to my wife, as I took the bird from inside my shirt, 'put this little one in with the others.'

She stared at it and said: 'What's that you've got?'

'It's a wild duckling,' I said.

'Where did you get it?' she said suspiciously.

I told her and she nearly went out of her mind on the spot. 'Take it out of the house,' she said, after spitting on the floor and making the sign of the cross between herself and the wild creature. 'It's enchanted. You had no right to touch it. You'll bring a curse on the house.'

I reasoned with her, saying that I would have been much more likely to bring a curse on the house by letting a helpless little bird die for want of warmth and nourishment.

'It was lucky for me that I brought it home,' I said, 'because the curse would surely fall on me if I left it where it was, to be devoured by a heathen weasel or a hawk. It would then. It would fall right down on top of me and I'd deserve it, for refusing to help a defence-less little bird.'

When I put it to her that way, she got calm and changed her mind about letting the wild duckling stay in the house.

'Since you didn't steal it from its mother,' she said, 'or lay a violent hand on it, there can be no harm in keeping it under our roof. I'll put it in the box with the others.'

The news soon spread through the village that we had a wild bird from 'The Enchanted Water' staying with us. The people came running from all directions to have a look at it. They were very disappointed when they saw it feeding out of a little trough on the kitchen floor with the tame ones. The wild creature had already made itself at home and the other orphans had taken kindly to the foundling.

'It doesn't look enchanted at all,' the people said. 'You could hardly tell the difference between it and the others. It's just an ordinary little black duckling.'

The wild one was a little quicker in its movements and a shade darker in colour, maybe than the tame ones. That was all the difference you could notice. In any case, the very young and the very old, among human beings as well as among other creatures, all look alike and behave alike, no matter how much they may differ in race or breeding.

'Of course it doesn't look enchanted,' I said, ' and there's no reason why it should. It's a holy creature, as can easily be seen by its gentleness and its good nature.'

When I told them how I had found it and why I took it home with me, they all agreed that I had done the right thing.

'It's a holy creature, all right,' they admitted, 'and there is no enchantment attached to it. Happy for you! It seems that the saint has given you one of his birds to foster.'

It was not very long, however, before the foundling began to show clear signs that it was different from the others and that its wild nature could not be tamed. It became more and more suspicious with each day that passed. It was always on guard. Instead of getting used to my wife and myself, it took to avoiding us in every possible way. It resisted all our efforts to make friends with it. It had a horror of being touched and of being hemmed into a corner. When summer came and my wife put the clutch out into a shed that had a small yard around it, we could hardly catch sight of the wild creature at all. It always ran when it heard one of us approach and it wouldn't touch its food while we were in the yard.

'It won't be long with us now,' I said to my wife. 'As soon as its wings are strong enough to take the high air, it will be heading for "The Enchanted Water" where it belongs.'

'It would be a pity,' my wife said, 'to let him go and he such a lovely bird. From a drake like that, we could get a new breed of ducks that would astonish the whole countryside. Do you think it would be a sin to clip his wings, so that he couldn't fly away.'

True enough, the foundling was growing into a beautiful drake, whose shining feathers were dotted with all the gay colours of the rainbow. He was a sight that brought gladness to the heart, through the splendour of his body and the supple quickness of his movements. I didn't blame my wife for being tempted to covet him. Even so, I wouldn't hear of her suggestion.

'Is it talking of laying a violent hand on a holy creature you are?' I said to her. 'Shame on you! It would be a terrible sin to clip his wings and deprive him of a power that was bestowed by God.'

'Maybe it would,' she said, 'but it would be a far greater sin to let him go before he has left us a clutch of his kind.'

'Let him go when he feels like it,' I said. 'It's not for us to stop him by means of sinful tricks.'

Then my wife smiled in a peculiar way and said: 'Maybe he won't be in such a hurry to leave us after all.'

'What do you mean?' I said to her.

'I think,' she said, 'that he has taken a great liking to one of our ducks. It's that slender little thing that's almost as black and shining as himself. They've always been together and he's terribly jealous of her. So, maybe it won't be necessary to clip his wings. That little black duck can't fly very far.'

Begob, she was right. The wild drake doted on the little black duck. Not only did he hardly ever leave her side, but he wouldn't let anybody else come near her. Even when his wings got so strong that he could fly high and far, he showed no sign of wanting to leave us for good. No matter how far away he flew, he always came back again and settled down beside his comrade. With his beak near the ground and his wings hanging, he chattered to her excitedly, as if he were giving her an account of his adventures. It seemed that he was bound to our yard by a chain far stronger than any ever fashioned by the hand of man: the golden chain of love.

When summer passed and the first big autumn rains

began to flood the marsh below the village, our ducks went almost mad with joy. They were off at dawn, just as soon as my wife let them out of their yard, to spend all day swimming about the flooded marsh and foraging in its muddy water that was thick with small fry of all sorts. My wife had to keep calling and calling them at sundown before they paid heed to her and came home.

It was then I realized that the wild drake was planning to take his comrade away with him. Day after day he worked from morning to night, teaching her to swim and fly as well as himself. When she got tired by her exertions and refused to obey him, he whacked her mercilessly about the head with his beak. Then again he would wheedle and coax her, until he persuaded her to do as she was bid. 'Faith, it wasn't long before she could fish under water like a cormorant and fly a good distance, too, fairly high up in the air. The two of them were always the last to come home. Even in the yard, they now kept entirely apart from the others. The little black duck was beginning to be just as suspicious and wary as her drake.

'Do you see what he's doing to her?' I said to my wife. She'll soon be as wild as he is. Then he'll take her away with him.'

'Have no fear,' my wife said. 'That little duck knows what's good for her. She won't leave her comfortable home.'

She was wrong that time, because we got up one morning a few weeks later to find that the wild drake and his comrade were missing from the yard.

'They've gone,' I said, 'and I knew they would be. I awoke in the night and heard wild geese cackling as they flew along the roof of the sky towards "The Enchanted Water." It was the cackling of the wild geese that sent them on their way. We've lost him now and our little black duck as well.'

'Have no fear,' my wife said, 'our little black duck will be glad to come back, after she has spent a few nights on that perishing lake. Then the drake will follow her back to the yard.'

My wife was wrong again, because the black duck never came back. Indeed, we got no tale or tidings for many months of the couple that had eloped. Many and many a time that winter as I searched for them all round the shores of the lake, high and low, I thought they had been carried off into enchantment. It was hard not to believe it, listening to the forlorn cries of the curlews re-echo through the cliffs and the sad whispering of the reeds rising up through the mist, like voices from the other world chanting a lament.

Then spring came and I finally discovered them one fine April morning, when the sunlight was dancing on the lake and the sky was full of singing larks. I was standing over there near 'The Heron's Rock' when I saw them come out of the hole in the cliff. The drake came out first and looked about him carefully after he had settled on the water. Then he called the duck. She flitted down gently, carrying two little ducklings on her back. She dropped them on the water beside the drake and went back into the cave for two more. She went back a second time for the fifth and last of her clutch.

LOVERS

It was extremely hot. Old Michael Doyle had been to the shop to get an ounce of tobacco. Now he found it difficult to make his way home. Leaning heavily on his stick, he walked slowly along under the shelter of a high wall that lined the road.

'I'm sorry now,' he grumbled, 'I didn't send one of the youngsters to fetch it.'

About a minute later he halted, straightened himself, and added:

'But they might have kept the money. Aw! 't's terrible the way I'm treated in what used to be my own house. Aw! I had better sit down and have a smoke. God almighty! Isn't it hot?'

He was seventy-seven years old. He had once been a man of great size, but now he was huddled together, an ungainly heap, as if all his limbs had been broken and disjointed and then stitched haphazard. His nose was a lump, his lower lip had drawn together in a bun, and his bleary eyes, through constant running, had made drains down his cheeks. His clothes were patched in an astonishing way. They did not fit and had obviously been cast off by his son and grandchildren. One of his grandsons was thirty years of age.

With great difficulty he sat down under the shelter of the wall. When he stretched out his legs and crossed his feet, the shadow of the wall reached halfway down his thighs. That was good. The upper part of his body was quite cool, and he sighed with content.

'Aye!' he said. 'It's a mortal terror how strength leaves a person.'

He fumbled in his pocket for his pipe. It had got entangled in his handkerchief, so that came out too, and with it everything that was in that pocket. He dropped the handkerchief beside him on the grass that grew under the wall. Then he got his knife out of the other pocket of his waistcoat. He spent more than two minutes trying to open it, and finally succeeded in doing so by placing the edge of the blade against the sharp corner of a stone in the wall.

'Hoich!' he said with pleasure. 'I'm not dead yet. Wasn't that clever now?'

Then he began to clean the bowl of his pipe. He blew through the stem. It whistled. It was clear. Putting the pipe down beside him on the grass he searched in his pockets for the ounce of tobacco he had just bought. It was nowhere to be found. He took off his hat and looked into the crown, without success, even though he fumbled under the band and pawed all over. He opened his waistcoat and then his shirt. He searched about his chest. The tobacco was nowhere. Then he got excited and began to get to his feet, crying angrily:

'That robber didn't give it to me. She took money and kept the tobacco.' As he was getting up, he put his hand on the handkerchief he had dropped. There was a hard lump under it. He cried: 'Ha! Here it is. Who'd ever think of it?'

So he settled himself down again, but in the effort to do so he dislodged the tobacco and he sat on it. When he examined the handkerchief there was nothing in it.

'Oh! Well!' he said. 'There's devilry in this.'

He began to scratch his head and then again set about looking for the tobacco, prodding the grass with his stick and clawing with his hands.

An old woman called Mary Kane, passing in the opposite direction, halted to watch him. She was seventy years old, but quite brisk. Her face was withered, like and old apple, but she still retained all her faculties. She wore boots with very high heels. It was obvious that she had once very beautiful legs and her carriage was that of a woman who was once beautiful. She wore a cashmere shawl that trailed down her back, almost to the ground, in a triangle, with the apex at her heels. In spite of the heat, she wore the shawl right out over her head, almost hiding her face.

She halted in front of the old man and then, recognizing him, she threw back her shawl and made a dramatic gesture with her arms.

'Bless my soul!' she said. 'If it isn't Michael Doyle. Ah! Musha, how are you, brother?'

The old man looked up slowly, shaded his eyes, and said:

'God and Mary to you. What village are you from?'

'Arrah! Don't you know me?' she said.

'Pooh!' said the old man. 'I don't know a person these days. They do be making fun of me. What village did you say?'

'D'ye mean to say ye don't know Mary Kane?'

'Oho!' said the old man. 'Is that who you are? Well now! And how is everybody belonging to you?'

'Aren't you the artful creature?' she said. 'Don't you know well I live alone and that I have nobody belonging to me, God help us?'

'Oho!' said the old man. ' 'Faith, I don't know you at all.'

'Oh!' said the old woman, throwing out her arms. 'Isn't he artful? And what are you looking for, may I ask?'

'Eh? What would I be looking for?'

'I saw you pawing about on the grass.'

'Begob, strangers are curious. And what would you be watching me for?'

'You're a sour old devil, Michael Doyle.'

'Why wouldn't I be sour when I just lost my tobacco?'

'Haw!' she said, jamming her arms against her hips and shaking herself with violence. 'Sure I knew you had lost something, and that you were pawing about for it, like a newborn infant, God help you; it's back you're going to the cradle, you that were the pride of the parish.'

'Begob,' he said, 'whoever you are, you have the gift of the gab. But it's strange anyways. A minute ago I had it in me hand. And now the devil has swallowed it.'

'Let me search,' she said.

'Search away,' he said. 'You won't find a grain of it.'

The old woman peered about sharply on the grass.

'What this?' she said, picking up a button. 'Did it fall of your waistcoat?'

He peered at it.

'It's a button,' he said. 'I found it and I'm keeping it for a young fellow. They like buttons. I do keep buttons and give them to the children. Then they go messages for me. It's cheaper that way than pennies.'

'It's nowhere to be seen,' she said. 'I declare to God, but I bet you're sitting on it. Move your old bones.'

She pushed him aside and found the tobacco, half buried in the grass. She held it up before his eyes in triumph. He grabbed it from her without a word of thanks. Having found his knife, he began to pare off some of the tobacco into the palm of his hand. She sat down beside him on her heels. He paid no attention to

her, but began to fill his pipe. She watched him closely
with her lips drawn back from her teeth and her eyes
narrowed, after the manner of people who are in the
habit of looking long distances out to sea. Then she
said:

'Now tell me on your soul, Michael, don't you know
me?'

He looked at her sourly and said:

'Begob, you're a great woman for arguing, so you
are.'

'I declare he doesn't know me,' she said plaintively.
'Oh! isn't this life cruel? It's five years since I saw you
last, Michael, and you knew me then although you
passed me by with a sour nod of salutation, same as
you always did since my marriage. Even the misfortunes
that I suffered didn't soften you. And now your
memory has gone completely. Like grass in a flooded
field it's buried under the weight of years. Ah! Sure it
breaks my heart to see you so, all withered like a rooted
bush. And I that can remember the day when you had
golden curls on your head and your eyes glittered like
the sea with the sun full on it. Aye! Death should come
young to the unfortunate. They are foolish who weep
over a young corpse. For it's an unholy sight you are,
all crippled and not knowing me.'

Unheeding, the old man cracked a match and put
it to his pipe and sucked, making a great noise each
time his hollowed cheeks expanded. Smoke belched
from the pipe. When it was well lit he hurled the match,
spat and wiped his mouth on his sleeve. All his movements were uncomely. Yet the old woman watched him
with a queer longing in her faded eyes.

'This is queer talk you have, woman,' he said gloomily.

'Who are you anyway? You're from a strange village,
I'm thinking.'

The old woman drew her shawl about her head once
more and sniffed. She put a corner of her apron to

her eyes. Taking his pipe out of his mouth, the old man looked at her closely. Then he spat, mumbled something, and pulled his hat further down over his eyes. The old woman began to rock gently.

'Not like you,' she said, 'my memory gets sharper with old age. Like a sick nerve it stabs me when I'm least expecting and then I go dreaming sadly through the years. Sure the first day I set eyes on you is as plain to me as the wall's black shadow on the road there. I was milking the cows when you came by on a horse in the evening. You blessed me and I looked up and then you stopped your horse and we began to talk, and I gave you warm milk to drink out of the can. Musha! There and then I belonged to you. Don't you remember that evening?'

'Oho!' said the old man. 'What evening are you talking about?'

'Musha, don't you remember how we used to meet on the hill above my father's house, how I used to run up the little road after nightfall and you used to be waiting for me?'

'Pooh!' said the little man. 'The devil a bit o' me remembers anything o' the kind. There now. Sure I hardly ever stir out of the house. Me waiting for ye!'

'Sure it's not today or yesterday I'm talking about,' she said, 'but this fifty-four years ago. I remember it well. I was sixteen, and you were just turned twenty-three. Poor man, it's all the drinking and fighting you did that brought you to this crippled state.'

'Arrah! Be easy with you,' he said. 'What drinking did I do? A few pints now and again. An odd glass of whiskey.'

'God forgive you,' she said. 'You were four times in jail, not to mention the time you came with your relations and stole me out of the house with a strong hand, and you gave Ned Kane such a beating with a stick that he spent three months in hospital and you got six months in jail for it.'

'Who? Me?' he said, taking his pipe out of his mouth and looking at her intently. 'Me in jail? What for?'

'For nearly killing Ned Kane with a stick that night you took me.'

The old man's face suddenly lit with a gleam of memory. He opened his mouth and then brought his right hand down heavily on his knee.

'Aw!' he said, with great emphasis. 'Ned Kane. I remember the dirty scoundrel. Hah! Musha, the devil take him. If I hit him he deserved it. A dirty scoundrel from head to foot. Begob then, I did beat him and I beat him well.'

He groped for his stick, clutched it, and said excitedly

'By my soul! I don't care who's listening, but I'll say this much: There was a day when I could beat with my bare hands any man in this parish that ever sucked at his mother's breast.'

'But don't you remember the night you came to the house.'

'Eh?' said the old man.

He scratched his head and still looked at her intently with his rheumy eyes. But his face gradually grew vacant and he said:

'Well, now ye drove it all out of my head again with your talk. Ech! I get dizzy with this heat. They do be making fun of me about it. I put down my hat and I declare to God I can't find it a minute after.'

'Ah! God help you, poor man,' she said wearily. 'But sure it's me that is to be pitied more. Maybe if I had you in our youth it wouldn't be. There'd be the care of children to soften the falling years. There it is. Every bit of it is plain to me, alive like a blister. You came then with your uncle and two men from your village to ask for me, and my father gave you the door. "Is it a drunkard that hasn't a shirt on his back I'd give my daughter?" said he. We had four cows then, and we were rich, and it was well known that I had thirty acres of land and the stock and two hundred gold sovereigns for my portion. That's how it was. It was to Ned Kane he wanted to give me, and it was Ned I married in spite of everything.'

'Tare an' ouns,' said the man crossly. 'My pipe is gone out.'

'Let it be,' she said, 'and listen to me. Though you don't remember, or pretend you don't, whichever it is, I'll tell you the truth now, for it's my first opportunity in all these years. When they wanted to marry me to Kane, I came and told you, and you said you'd take me, if the devil was sitting on my bed counter. So there it was. Ned Kane came with his people, and they were in the house making the match, when all of a sudden there was a clatter of horses outside, and you called out. It was dead of night. "Come out, Ned Kane," says you, "or faith you'll come out a corpse." Your uncle Peter Timoney, was with you and Simon Grealish and Hugh Rody and more men, too. Then you burst in the door and laid out whatever was there. Such shouting was never heard before or after. Then you barged into the room where I was with my mother and the women. My mother marked you with a tongs, but nothing could stop you that night. And glad enough I was to go, too. Then you took me away behind you on the horse, but sure when the priest was awakened at the dawn, he refused to marry us. Then the police came and we hiding at your uncle's house and every man was arrested. Back I was brought. Oh! that was the night. And d'ye mean to tell me, Michael Doyle, that you don't remember it?'

The old man paused with a lighted match to the bowl of his pipe. He looked up at her and then, without speaking, he drew at the pipe, lit it, and threw away the match.

'People do have a great talk of the fighting I done,'

he said. 'They're always casting it in my face. But I dare say I was no worse than others.'

He began to grumble while the old woman continued her story.

'You went to jail then,' she said, 'and when Kane came out of hospital we were married. What could I do? Sure I had no hand or part in it. I'd have gone with you anywhere. I used to cry my eyes out then. But there was nothing to be done. And, God forgive you, it was me you blamed for it. It's been a long and lonely life of misery I had, with Kane drinking and routing whatever there was, all he could lay his hands on, until he died of sickness. Not a child blessed my hearth, and hardly a relation is left to me now. And that's the way it is. Nor you left to me either; nothing only a sad, sad memory of a love that was strangled in its cradle.'

She sobbed and rocked herself, with her shawl far out over her eyes. The old man moved about restlessly, looking at her from time to time, mumbling to himself. At last he said:

'Poor woman, you have your sorrow.'

'Aye,' she said. 'It's a load I carry with me always. This talking has made it heavier. I wish I passed you by.'

She got to her feet, shook herself and straightened out her shawl. She dried her eyes with her apron. Then she threw back her shawl and looked at him. Her eyes were red and her lips twitched.

'Won't you say a gentle word to me,' she said, 'before I go my road?'

He looked up at her stupidly.

'God bless you!' he said.

'And you, Michael,' she answered. 'May you rest in peace!'

She turned and walked away, her shawl in a triangle, her high heels tipping the road sharply. He looked after her, pulling slowly at his pipe.

His withered countenance seemed to have lost all traces of human conciousness. It was apelike. His rheumy eyes, wrinkled like those of a gorilla, had no light in them.

'Pooh!' he said after a while. 'What was that poor woman saying?'

He sat with his mouth wide open for another few minutes, as if trying to remember something. But his mind was a complete blank. Then he struggled to his feet and trudged homewards, walking on the grass by the wall in the shadow.

THE FLOOD

The river swelled silently. Thick rain pattered softly without a pause. The willows on either bank grew corpulent as their stems disappeared beneath the rising water. Swirling eddies made sudden sucking sounds, as the increasing belly of the river tried to squeeze through the archway of the bridge. Corks, sticks, and leaves came whirling down, diving and bobbing. At dawn only the tips of the reeds were visible.

Then the tips of the reeds disappeared. The river overflowed its banks and trickled through the naked brown tree roots, on to the green grass of the fields on either side. To left and right of the bridge foam gathered, and swift streams ran along the base of the brick wall. These streams increased rapidly as the archway cut the excess from the river's girth and sent it frothing to left and right. The fields were being submerged.

Then a great flight of living things began. As soon as the grey cold light of the autumn sun dispelled the darkness of the night, myriad forms of life appeared on the green uneven surface of the fields, crawling and rushing in terror, flying from the water that approached silently from the river, making only tiny sogging sounds as it trickled through the surface earth and through the lean grass and among the roots of the field weeds.

The flight began from the river banks. But it spread away rapidly upwards along the gentle slope of the fields. Each tiny fleeing insect roused the next, until the surface of the fields was one moving mass of black and brown and green bodies, squirming and rushing and twisting in the varied and agonising forms of their flight.

Whither? Here, there, back and forth, an ignorant, frenzied rout of tiny things. They struggled blindly. They clawed and bit and crushed mercilessly. Each was for itself. They dashed heedlessly into roots, maiming their rain-sodden legs. Overthrown as they rushed through a channel between two thick roots, a score of different species lay on their backs, kicking the moist air with their tiny legs, while others crawled and rushed over them. Strong, tall blades of grass became towers, up which hundreds crawled to escape the flood. And wriggling bodies, dislodged from the summit of a blade, hurtled through the air, to the fields, as from a tall precipice to their death.

The river swelled. The banks disappeared. The flood covered the fields along either bank. Only ridges of green grass were left here and there, like islands, covered with a feverish horde of insects, cut off from retreat, waiting, insensibly for the inevitable approach of the flood, struggling and devouring one another as they waited.

Amidst the scum and debris floating on the water, masses of drowned insects whirled along, dead, dying, dismembered.

And each twig and piece of jetsam was a raft, covered with fierce things fighting for their lives, burrowing into clefts, clinging in silence.

The debris was carried down on the stream. It halted at the bridge, carried to left and right by the swirling currents. The currents jammed it into a mass on either side of the bridge, against the brick wall. Twigs interlaced with yellow and green scum formed a platform, and each fleck of froth, swimming down the slow tide over the fields, rushed into it, increasing it. A wall of yellowish froth rose gradually around each platform.

Cargo after cargo of insects was carried into each wall of froth by the current. Some twigs were caught by under currents, sucked beneath the water, and their loads were drowned. Others were jammed in the outer wall of froth, and the weakened insects, entangled in the froth, perished from exhaustion. Only the larger twigs swung straight into the press of the debris with their loads intact.

Then a terrific struggle commenced. A great mass of insects tried to climb up the brick wall. Insects that had legs clambered up first. They easily gripped the rough surface of the bricks. The first ones immediately dived into crevices. The crevices filled. The mass pressed farther up. The wall was black with rushing things.

The green crawling insects found it impossible to gain a grip on the wall. They were too slow. Hanging on to their twigs with their tails, they raised their twisting heads into the air and then swayed forward, dabbing uncertainly at the wall with their snouts. But the movement of the current allowed the twigs only a solitary moment against the wall before they were tossed away again. So that the green serpents, reaching out for the wall, lost their balance when the twigs were tossed. They were cast into the current and drowned. The scum-covered debris was a living mass of writhing green things; strange, half-formed, primeval things, tossing their heads in the air hopelessly.

The rain ceased at noon, but the river continued to swell, draining the surfeit of water from the neighbouring earth. The flood rose higher. The insects were driven up the brick wall. They struggled upwards until they lay in a long thick line beneath the cement coping, like a living tide mark.

Of the myriad things that had fled in the night only a few thousand remained. Of those survivors, some died of exhaustion and hunger during the day. They lost their hold and fell down into the water. Others, rendered desperate by hunger, surmounted the wall and descended into the roadway beyond, only to perish in the water that covered it. But the remainder stayed without movement under the coping, with their bellies jammed tight to the wall, clinging miserly to every shred of their vitality, in their great instinctive battle with the flood.

At midnight the flood reached its highest point. Then it began to fall back into the river bed. The next morning a bright sun appeared. The flood decreased all day. At sunset the river banks appeared. Next morning the fields were emptied of water. The river flowed sourly between its shabby banks, after its grand gesture.

Then the insects disbanded from their shelter. Slowly, cautiously, they moved down the wall into the soggy fields. On dry ground again, among their accustomed grasses and roots and weeds, they bustled about savagely, seeking food and strength.

From all sides hordes of insects advanced towards the river in the wake of the flood, devouring the rich food left like a rash on the earth's face.

THE SALTED GOAT

The peasants of the village of Kilmillick are peculiar people. Their village is the most remote and primitive village in Inverara. No stranger ever penetrates there except an occasional Jew who comes to peddle shoddy cloth, or an archaeologist who comes examining the crags and glens for traces of its prehistoric inhabitants. It is so close to the high cliffs and the Atlantic that seagulls often fly down to the village roofs to devour the fish they have caught in the sea, and in winter sea froth falls like snow on the cabins. So that the people of the village are sadfaced, peaceful and given to the practice of strange superstitions.

At times strange things are reported to have happened there, such as Mick Hernon's red cow having a calf with a fish's tail and the fairies carrying a newborn child out of old Mrs. Derrane's arms as she was nursing it by the kitchen fire. But, of course, old Mrs. Derrane might have been slightly tipsy when the child fell in the fire and the whirlwind that came in the door at the time is nothing unusual in Kilmillick, because of the cross currents caused by the surrounding hills, and the calf may have been born prematurely. But Patsy Halloran's salted goat was undoubtedly a fact witnessed and verified not only by the peasants of the village, but by the parish priest and the police sergeant.

Halloran lived alone on the eastern outskirts of the village in a tumbledown cabin. The rotting thatch sagged inwards in the middle, so that the ropes that bound it stood out several inches from the straw. The unpainted door was pockmarked with stones thrown at it by the village urchins, who were in the habit of persecuting Patsy, because he was old and poor and had no important relatives. It was falling outwards at the top, torn loose from the hinge. The stone walls had once been whitewashed, but they had gone yellow in large streaks, and the strips of mortar between the stones were visible. The single pane of glass in the single window was broken and stuffed with a piece of brown bag. And the squat stone chimney was the resting-place of starlings and seabirds, so that one often saw a dogfish head perched there as if it were the shore of some wild sea.

There was but one room, where Patsy slept, ate and rested. There was a low wooden bed in one corner, a dresser opposite the fireplace, and a small table between the dresser and the bed. Then there was Patsy himself and the yellow goat. The goat lived in the cabin and was Patsy's sole companion, for the villagers never visited him or held any intercourse with him, except to bid him the time of the day when he passed, on his way to or from his six sheep that he fed on ten acres of land on the broad crag south of the Yellow Cliff. Myles's Crag the peasants call it, because it is said some prehistoric Myles strangled a sea-serpent there that had come up from the sea to devour him.

Nobody in the village knew how long the yellow goat had been in the cabin, for the peasants had only vague ideas of the passing of the years. They said the goat was there since the year Stephen Feeney's horse died of the thirst. But what year that was nobody remembers. And the goat never had a kid, and as a consequence never provided Patsy with any milk, so that he had to depend on the charity of the old woman next door for some cow's milk to colour his tea. And the old woman always crossed herself when she left Patsy's cabin, for she thought the goat was an evil spirit. Nor could one blame the poor woman, for the goat had a peculiar expression in her yellow eyes, an expression like that of some wise old philosopher who knows that the world is full of sorrow and folly and holds himself aloof and cool while all the rest of mankind rush about worrying over trifles. But, then, all goats have that peculiar expression in their eyes, and Patsy's goat was not unusual in that respect. Neither was there anything else unusual about her, the long matted yellow hair on her haunches, or the way she had of getting on her hind legs and undoing the latch of the door when she wanted to enter or leave the cabin, or the way she had of rubbing herself against Patsy's legs when he was sitting by the fire. All tame goats do things like that. But the old woman told these habits of the goat to the neighbours, and the neighbours put their heads together and said that the goat was the spirit of Patsy's wife, who had died the year before he got the goat. And the men laughed and said that old Patsy was out of his mind 'an' that's all there's to it.'

And without a doubt Halloran had been a trifle insane for a good many years. For it would be difficult for a man to live alone in the village of Kilmillick and not go insane. But his insanity was more akin to that of the ancient hermits who clothed themselves in sackcloth and ashes and went to live in a desert among wild beasts and birds, than to the insanity of sane people who cause suffering to their fellow-creatures by cunning and avarice. Robins, blackbirds, sparrows and starlings came to his door in the morning to be fed, and they would perch on his hand or on his tattered old hat, that had a cord around it to keep it on his head. And even when the little boys threw stones at him and followed him imitating a goat, he reprimanded them kindly and never lost his temper. Once, however, he did lose his temper, and gave Tim Hernon's young son a sound thrashing, when he caught him persecuting the yellow goat near the cabin. The boy had the goat on her back and was tying a cord on her hind leg, so that it would eat into the flesh and be impossible to remove until the goat lost her leg. But apart from that he was kindness itself. His insanity manifested itself in his habit of talking aloud to himself or to the goat, and when he was walking along the road he often picked up a pebble, spat on it and threw it over his head. When he went to the well for water he walked around it three times bare-headed before he baled water from the stream, and when he was sitting late at night on his three-legged stool before the little turf fire that was dying on the hearth, he would suddenly bare his yellow teeth and break into loud laughter for no reason whatsoever. Then, just as suddenly, he would strike his breast and burst into silent tears. And at those times the yellow goat would rub against his legs, making dismal noises. And she usually comforted him. Halloran would look at her, stroking his greyish brown beard that grew half-way down his throat, with his long wrinkled face as yellow as parchment, and nod his head. Then he would catch his left ear, that was shrunken to half the size of the right ear, with both hands and say to the goat, 'It's here all the trouble is, Peg; this ear is the cause of it.'

Then, one winter's night, when the Atlantic breakers were making wild music as they lashed against the towering cliffs and the storm wind was bellowing over the crags, with a myriad bubbles of sea froth flying before it like blossoms torn from a garden in the sky, and the sea-birds whirled over the village screaming, Patsy awoke with a start. He heard the goat shriek in his sleep. He called to her and got no reply. Then he hurriedly lit a candle, and when the flickering light spread around the kitchen he saw the old goat lying on her side in the middle of the kitchen, with her side heaving. She was breathing her last, and her yellow eyes were looking at him sadly. And then, as if she had been waiting to look at him for the last time, she snorted, tried to moan, stiffened her legs and lay still. She was dead.

Halloran stood for a long time in his shirt, holding the candle in his hand, looking at her. His yellow face lit up by the light had a pitiful expression in it. 'Ah,' he muttered, 'Ah! ah! Now everything has left me. Everything.' And he sat on the edge of the bed shivering until it was broad daylight. Then he dressed himself, took the cabin door off its hinges and placed it on the floor. He put the goat on the door and skinned her. He cut her in small pieces, put her in a tub and salted her. He placed the tub in front of the hearth. He put the door back on its hinges and bolted it. He put a board to cover the window on the inside, so as to shut out all light. Then he sat on his three-legged stool looking at the tub that contained the goat.

He sat there four days, until all the turf he had in the cabin was burned and his food was eaten. He had more turf and potatoes and dried fish in the little hut attached to the eastern gable of the house, but he would not go out to get it. Neither would he open the door to the old woman who came with his milk every evening towards nightfall. 'The fairies will fly away with Peg if I leave her,' he said to himself. And the old woman said to herself, 'Old Patsy is in the tantrums, so I better stop away for a bit.'

And she did stay for a whole week. The first man to come near the cabin was the parish priest, trying to persuade Halloran to go to confession. He knocked at the door and received no answer. He shouted. No answer. He made enquiries of the old woman. No, she hadn't seen Patsy for a fortnight. He came back, followed by the old woman and a few of the neighbours and forced in the door. The kitchen was in terrible disorder. Every stick of furniture, including the bed, had been burned. All except the tub which lay in front of the hearth. And beside it lay Halloran stiff in death.

When the police sergeant came he found a strip of blanket between Halloran's teeth. 'The poor man died of the hunger,' said the sergeant.

But the villagers swear that the goat was a devil and that Patsy had sold himself to her.

THE WHITE BITCH

A peasant and his wife were walking along the crags towards the cliffs. A little white bitch, wagging her tail and with her nose to the ground, ran along in front of them, hunting rabbits. Now and again she would pause, lift a forepaw and sniff at the air. There was a black spot on her right flank and another on her left ear.

The peasant walked with his hands clasped behind his back, looking at the ground. His wife walked behind him knitting. They never spoke until they reached the brink of the cliff. Then the peasant spat into the sea, hitched his belt, and said, 'Well, I suppose in the name of God I might as well do what's to be done. Here, Topsy. Come here, Topsy. Good doggie.'

The woman looked away and brushed her eyes with a corner of the shawl that was tied around her neck and shoulders. The bitch came up at a gallop, snapping at a wasp that circled around her head. She lay on her belly at the peasant's feet, looking up into his face with moist eyes. He bent down and caught her by the back of the neck. She rolled over on her side, put her two forepaws around his hand, and licked it. Then she began to whine and shiver.

The man let go his hold and stood up. 'To hell with it for a story; I can't drown her!' he said. 'You are a devil of a woman to ask me to drown her.'

The woman stamped her foot and shook her knitting in his face. 'Hey, what's that yer saying?' she said. 'Why don't ye go an' earn seven and sixpence then to pay for her licence? If you hadn't drunk the price of the pig ye'd have money now to pay for her.'

The man began to swear and walk about. The bitch crawled after him, licking his legs. 'Couldn't we sell a bushel of potatoes to the schoolmaster?' he said at length. 'He was asking me the other day...'

'Don't be silly, you fool. What are the two young pigs going to live on? Throw her down, and don't stand there like an old woman.'

The man scratched his head and spat out again. 'The devil a drown,' he said. 'I'll hide her where the police won't see her.'

'Yerra is it out of yer mind ye are, man? There isn't a neighbour but would be running to the police this very evening with information. Throw her down, silly, or if you are too cowardly to do it, I'll throw her down myself.'

The man swore and bent down to the bitch suddenly. He seized her by the back of the neck and by the tail. The bitch began to howl and clawed at the ground. He raised her up, swung her twice backwards and forwards, and then hurled her out over the cliff. The bitch sailed through the air with her tail and legs extended and her head bent. Then she disappeared.

The woman threw her apron over her face and began to weep aloud. 'My poor little dog,' she cried. 'If you hadn't drunk the price of the pig, we'd have her yet to comfort us.'

'Child of misfortune,' shouted the man; 'If you don't mend your ways I'll throw you down after her.'

'Brute. That's what you are.'

The man caught his hat and threw it on the ground.

'Ah, John' said the woman suddenly softening, 'I didn't mean what I said. 'Tis I was the cause of it.'

'Of course, you were the cause of it. Ye're the cause of every misfortune.'

'Look down, John and see is she dead. Maybe she isn't dead. It's no more than forty feet and the tide is in. She must have fallen in the water. If she didn't strike a rock she's not killed.

'Look down yourself, if you want to. She's drowned now, and may the devil devour her.' He began to walk away slowly.

The woman ran to the brink of the cliff and, going on her knees, she looked down. 'Oh, John, John,' she shouted, 'she's not dead. Come here. See she's shaking herself down on that rock. Don't you hear her barking? I declare she's trying to climb up the cliff. Come here, John. Look. Look.'

The man ran excitedly to the brink and looked down. 'I declare to God she's alive,' he said. 'More's the pity. Now she'll have to die there of the hunger. I was a fool not to tie a stone to her neck. It was all your fault any way with your nagging.'

The two of them leaned over the cliffs on their hands and knees, looking down for some time. The bitch saw them and began to bark loudly, and scraped at the base of the cliff. A little stream of blood was running down her right knee over the white skin, and she was shivering after her dive into the cold sea. Both the peasant and his wife were on the verge of tears looking at her. 'Begob I'd give all my fifteen acres of land to have her up here again,' said the man at last, 'the poor devil is human. 'Tis only a wild savage would hurt a poor animal like it for the sake of seven and sixpence. But it's done now and may the devil mend it. We'll have no luck.'

'Oh God between us and all harm,' said the woman,

'd'ye hear the pitiful whine of her? It cuts into my heart like a knife. John, John go and get a boat at the shore beyond and bring her ashore. And I'll go this very night and sell the five yards of cloth I had for a dress to Kate Mahoney. I'll get ten shillings for it and I'll give ye a shilling for a drink. Do, and may God reward ye.'

The man jumped to his feet and said,

'Fool, argue with a woman, argue with the devil,' and he stalked away to the shore westwards.

The woman kept calling to the bitch and crying. The bitch had now sat on her haunches and began to howl at the sky piteously. Then she began to limp around on three legs, licking her wounded knee. Then she lay down at the base of the cliff and began to rub her head against it as if she were trying to caress it. She lay like that until the peasant came around the headland in his boat. She raised her head and began to bark joyously as she recognised him. Then she jumped into the sea and swam out to the boat. He pulled her up into the boat and caressed her in his arms lovingly.

THE PROCLAMATION

Some years ago, while the whole country was talking of the amazing circumstances connected with the Slackbally murder, the following statement was sent through the post to the officials who were connected with the trial, to the leading newspapers of Ireland, and to the Ministry of Justice. As the extraordinary document, in my opinion, tells the story of the murder with remarkable clarity, I give it here in full, without any further comment on my part:

To all whom it may concern

I, John Francis Considine, Brigade Commandant, here lay the whole facts of the case before the public, not because I'm getting the wind up, for I may tell you that my lines of communication are so strong that I defy the lot of you, but in order to defend my good name and the good name of my family and all connected with me, as soldiers and otherwise.

Here are the facts, going back a bit, so as to make everything clear, for a man has his sense of decency left no matter what his position may be, given to understand that he had one in the first case. To those that know, those belonging to my own town and county, and indeed to those connected with the national movement actively in the whole country, these facts would not be necessary; but, here and now, let every man, woman, and child in the country have my history, where I came from, how I got to where I did, and then how I fell, like many a man before me, through the callous ingratitude of people in high position.

Aspersions have been cast on my character because I fought in the British army during the Great War, but here I say, without any intention of apologizing for my actions, no matter when and what they were, that I was led astray by ulterior propaganda, which received the support of the parish priest and other prominent local people, now high in the counsels and fat on the loot of the nation. As the poet said, mine were the wounds and the hunger, theirs was the reason why. In any case, my father was a respected butcher in our town, and I received a good education, and my uncle hurled for the county the only time in the past twenty years they got as far as the All-Ireland semi-final. As far as I know, there was never a charge of any crime whatsoever laid at the door of any member of my family, from petty larceny to informing, but they were always in the van of whatever moonlighting or cattle driving there was to be done.

Here also I must say that in writing this statement, I have received the support of a public official connected with education, whose name and calling for obvious reasons must remain a secret, and that many corrections and addenda have been inserted on his behalf—otherwise I'd give more of my mind to some people, in language they could understand.

After being discharged from the armed forces of the foreign imperialist power, which until recently oppressed us and has still got its hostile eye on us, I plunged headlong into the national movement and during the wars of liberation rose to the rank of Brigade Commandant, rank corresponding to that of Brigadier

General in the British army. I made myself famous in the three neighbouring counties by acts of heroism. Then came the Civil War, when I faithfully served the new government, defending the honour of the nation against her internal enemies. But during these latter alarums and excursions, as the saying is, like many another poor fellow, I got too fond of the drink, the curse of God on it, it has ruined many a man. So the prime boys wouldn't have anything to do with me after the war was over and the enemy routed. So they chucked me a couple of hundred quid and told me to get into my civilian pants. Young scuts that never fired a shot and other fountain-pen warriors that served on the so-called staff are now up in Dublin drinking the champagne that men like me earned for them, while good men like myself are hiding in dugouts with a price on our heads. What was there left for me to do but drink in the hotel and talk to the boys? So the money went, and very shortly I found myself drinking on tick and thinking of going to America. God! I felt so sore I was ready for anything.

Well! One evening, and I in this state of mind, a man came into the snug of the hotel and found me sitting there alone. He was James Finnigan, formerly connected with the Royal Irish Constabulary as a sergeant. That he was allowed to live in the district, on terms of human equality with the people, after his association with that fell body, can be explained by the fact that he was understood to have served within the police as a spy for the national forces. Whether he was or not I cannot say. But in any case, a spy is a spy, and that is all there is to it. I never had any time for him, with his pointed moustaches and his skinny face and ferret eyes. He often used to sidle up to me, trying to make friends, but I generally kept him at a distance. This time anyway, I was broke and I had a thirst on me, and there was so much on the slate that I didn't like touching

Fred Connors for any more; so when Finnigan asked me to have one, I hadn't the heart to say no. We got talking, and after five or six drinks — you know the state a man gets into — I practically forget who he was. He was edging me nicely along, talking about how badly I was treated and the rest of it. Then finally he began to tell me the position he was in himself.

'Jack,' said he, 'I wish I had your courage with a gun'.

'Why?' said I.

'Well!' he said. 'By my solemn oath, there is only one way I can get myself out of the fix I am in, and that's by creasing somebody I won't name.

'Good God!' I said.

'It's the God's truth I'm telling you,' he said. 'I'm in debt up to my eyes with the developments I made on that farm I bought, and that foreman of mine is taking this very moment to press me for his wages, amounting to one hundred and ten quid.'

They were the words he used. The damn cheek of the man having a farm anyway. But what with the drink and everything else, I listened to him.

'D'ye mean Tommy Dillon?' I said, referring to the man that worked for him.

'The same,' he said. 'He's threatening to take the law of me. You know the position I'm in. It's easy enough to bring animus against me in the courts, because I had the misfortune to be connected with the Force.'

'I see,' said I. 'Won't he listen to reason?'

'No,' said Finnigan.

'Couldn't you put him off,' said I, 'with a few quid or something?'

'Not a penny less will he take than the full amount,' said Finnigan.

I did my best, drunk as I was, to put him off the deed he contemplated, but you might as well look for mercy from a stone. He was intent on the man's death.

So finally he said to me:

'I know I can rely on you Jack to keep the matter a secret if the proposition I'm going to make doesn't appeal to you.'

'I'm not an informer,' said I.

'Well! It's this way,' he said. 'I know Dillon is determined to ruin me. He wants to drive me and my wife and kids off that farm and take it for himself. It's either him or me for it. He must be got rid of, Jack, for the love o' God, could ye give us a hand?'

'How d'ye mean?' said I.

'Well' he said. 'I'm a poor man, but I could scrape together twenty-five quid for the man that would crease Dillon.'

I was so muddled with drink, God forgive me, that I didn't strike him where he sat, and of course there was no question of exposing his plot. I had no witnesses, even if I wanted to go to the police with the story, something that was far from my mind. So what could I do?

'I'll do it for ye,' said I, before I knew what I was saying.

He gripped my hand and damn near went on his knees to thank me, talking about his wife and children. He never thought of the fact that Dillon had a wife and children too. Neither did I until after, but I was muddled with drink. In any case, we drew up a plan of campaign and decided that the job was to be done at an agreed spot, where Dillon was in the habit of passing on his bicycle. He handed me over ten quid, and the remainder was to be paid as soon as the job was done. Then we had more drinks, and we parted for the night, I being in a state of intoxication.

Next morning I awoke with a bad head, and the first thing that came to my mind was the murder of Tommy Dillon which I had bargained to perform for Finnigan. There and then, I decided to place the matter in the

hands of Sergeant Kane of the Civic Guards, coming
to the conclusion that Finnigan was a man of criminal
inclination and a danger to the community. So I went
up to the barracks, brought the sergeant to one side
and told him all about it.

'We've got him,' cried Kane, slapping his thigh,
'We've got him now, if we manage it properly.'

'How d'ye mean?' said I.

Kane is a bit of a fool, although he thinks a lot of
himself, one of these big beef-necks that have more
guts than brains. He won't mind if I tell the world what
I think of him. I'd say the same thing to his face and
will say so in my own time, which is not now, for he
has got me into a power of trouble.

'Listen,' said he. 'Don't say a word to a soul, Jack,
about this. We have him nabbed for fair.'

'Who d'ye mean?' said I.

That dirty blackguard Finnigan,' said he. We have
our knife in him. He's eaten up with envy of the Guards;
so he goes around saying our discipline is nothing
compared to that of the old R.I.C. We'll settle him.
You go ahead now and go out with him to-night, just
the same as if nothing transpired here between us.'

'Good God!' said I. 'Sergeant Kane, is it inciting me
to murder you are?'

'Shut your big mouth,' said Kane. 'It's nothing of
the kind — sure you need only hit him on the legs, or
just fire in the air, provided — wait a minute. I have
a better idea. We better take Tommy Dillon himself in
on this too.'

Good Lord! I began to get terrified.

'Oh, look here now, Sergeant,' said I. 'This is getting
a bit thick for me. I don't want to be in a conspiracy.
I'm not that sort of a man. If you fellows are trying to
hang Finnigan, let it be done fair and square. Or if you
want to plug him, go to his house and do it, while he's
on his own floor. Take him out of bed, give him a

chance to say his prayers, and ram it into him in the old style. This Frenchy business is too much like British diplomacy. I'll have no hand or part in it.'

'You will, by God,' he said, 'or I'll write a report to headquarters about the statement you made here this morning.'

We damn near came to blows, for I'll take cheek from no man, much less a big tub of beef like Paddy Kane. But anyway we served on the same flying column together at the start of the trouble in the old times; so that was all there was to it. I agreed to do what he told me. During the day, we saw Tommy Dillon privately in a house up the road, and we put the case before him. It was all we could do to prevent Tommy from going after Finnigan on the spot with a pitchfork. Poor Tommy, he wasn't a bad old skin, and I'm sorry the way it turned out for him, but it was all Kane's fault, not to mention the murderer Finnigan. In any case, I'm paying the piper. No matter how it goes, it's exile for me. But the truth must be stated and my honour vindicated.

'Don't you do nothing of the kind, Tommy,' said Kane, when the lad was talking of the pitchfork. 'You'd only get hung for killing him and we'd be dragged in too, for it would come out in the evidence that we told you about his plot.'

'I'm agreed,' said Tommy at last.

Then we made our plans. The Sergeant and two men were to lie on one side of the road, at the spot I had chosen. Finnigan and myself were to be on the other side, and Tommy was to come along on his bicycle. And it all turned out that was as arranged. I met Finnigan after nightfall and we went along. He had a shotgun slung in parts under his overcoat, and I was carrying my automatic. We took up our position. After about a quarter of an hour, the night was fairly dark, we saw Tommy's bicycle lamp coming along, and he was whistling to himself. I suppose he had the wind up in any case.

'Come on, Finnigan,' said I. 'We better go out on the road and stop him for fear we might miss in the bad light.'

He was all excitement, and I could feel him trembling beside me. He was a cowardly man in any case. So we stepped out of the hedge without a word, just as Tommy was coming up.

'Blow him off the bike,' said I to Finnigan, as we came out, 'then I'll polish him off.'

Just at that moment, Sergeant Kane jumped up from behind the other side of the road and cried:

'Hands up, Finnigan, or I'll shoot you where you stand!'

Tommy Dillon dismounted and stood there in the middle of the road. Finnigan gave me one look — I'll never forget it — and then, as quick as lightning, he turned his shotgun on me, cried out, 'You bloody informer!' and fired. In his excitement and the darkness, he missed me, though I got a few grains in the shoulder. Then he turned and ran at Tommy.

God! I thought a red-hot iron bar was poked into my chest at that word 'informer'. So I just took aim at him and blazed away. The fool Tommy Dillon, instead of running away, had made a drive for Finnigan, as the latter approached. Poor Tommy's anger got the better of him. It was all a mix-up, but this is how it turned out. Finnigan emptied his second barrel right into Tommy's face and damn near blew his head clean off, and I struck Finnigan with the second round I fired straight in the heart, as luck would have it. He deserved it, but I rather somebody else did it. In any case, I was only trying to save Tommy's life. There they were both dead. Sergeant Kane came up to me and said, after we had examined the corpses:

'I'm sorry, Jack, but I'll have to place you under arrest.'

'I'll see you to Hell first,' I said, 'after you being responsible for the whole mess.'

So I struck him in the face with the muzzle of my gun and floored him.

'The first man that moves a hand,' I cried to the other two Guards, covering them, 'I'll shoot him dead.'

Then I picked up Tommy's bicycle and rode away. And that's the full story of the events leading up to the trial that has brought no credit to anyone, least of all to the accused, not in custody. And I may tell all whom it may concern, that the said accused is not going to be in custody as long as he and his faithful friends have got a round of ammunition left.

Indeed, I see now that the whole thing was a plot against me as well as against Finnigan — may God have mercy on the souls of those that were unfortunately made the victims of this miscarriage of justice.

I make a final appeal to my fellow countrymen and women, to see that the bloodhounds of injustice are taken off my tracks and to remember at this late hour the unfortunate man known as John Francis Considine, late Brigade Commandant and a soldier of the people who served his country faithfully and deserves a better reward than the gallows.

> *(Signed)* John Francis Considine
> Brigade Commandant (in hiding)

Naturally this astonishing document was never printed by any of the journals to which it was submitted. I myself was permitted to read a copy by a friend who was connected with the trial; but that was quite recently. At that time I could barely recall the case. Considine was never taken and indeed I might never have taken the trouble to publish the matter had I not recently met in New York a man who had seen Considine there. He told me that the former Brigade Commandant looked exceedingly prosperous and happy.

BOHUNK

With his slouch hat pulled far down over his brick-red boozy face and his hands clenched in the pockets of his heavy black overcoat, big Jack Fleming stared at the newborn greyhound pups for a long time in gloomy silence. Although generally ruthless and even brutally insensitive in his conduct, he always hated the decision that every breeder of race-dogs is forced to make when a litter is greater than the mother's capacity for nourishment.

To make matters worse, the little fawn bitch seemed to know what was in store for some of her brood. Lying on her side, she kept trying to hide the seven sleek and sightless creatures that crawled over her distended udder. At the same time, she looked up at Fleming with mute appeal in her watery eyes that still showed the pain of giving birth. Her nose twitched spasmodically and she rapped the straw with the tip of her curving tail.

Fleming suddenly cursed under his breath and then looked angrily at his kennel man.

'Speak up, Joe' he said. 'We can't stay here all day. What do you think, fellah? What have you got in mind?'

Stapleton was a tall lean man with bushy grey hair and a prominent Adam's apple. Just then, his emaciated bony face was lit by the strange smile of a mystic under the influence of occult revelation. His blue eyes were fixed and wide open. Unlike Fleming, who was a gambler above all else, the kennel man's sole ambition in life was to breed a super dog; a champion among champions.

'It all depends, Jack,' he said in the shrill and high-pitched voice of an excited girl. 'It all depends on whether you agree to keep that awkward-looking pup with the powerful legs.'

Then he thrust forward his right foot and touched one of the litter; a large and ungainly creature that already dominated the other six and had even managed to get proper hold of teat

'Are you crazy?' Fleming said. 'That fellow is a monster. He'll be the first to take the drink.'

'Hold on, Jack,' Stapleton insisted. 'Hold on now, like a good man. You can strike me dead where I stand, but I'll still swear with my last breath that you have the makings of a champion in that pup. For God's sake, look at his powerful legs. Look at the way he has made himself the boss of. . . '

'Shut up, Joe,' Fleming interrupted. 'I tell you he's a monster. In a thousand years, you couldn't make a good tracker out of that loutish creature. He looks like a mongrel dropped in there by mistake.'

The two men argued heatedly for a while and the bitch looked anxiously from one to the other; whining and twitching her little nose as if she understood every word that was being said.

'Have it you own way,' Stapleton said at length in a hurt tone.

Then Fleming got afraid of being forced to make the decision on his own account.

'Take it easy, Joe,' he implored. 'I'm only trying to say...'

'Have it your own way,' Stapleton shouted at the top of his voice, as he waved his battered hat, 'but you'll be drowning the chance of a lifetime. I have a hunch about that queer creature and my hunches are not often wrong; as you have good reason to know.'

'That's true enough, Joe,' Fleming said. 'There's no need to lose your temper. I know you're not often wrong and that your equal doesn't exist in judging pups. You have the knack, blast you, whether it's a knack or a gift. Who cares what it is? You have it, in any case. For the life of me all the same, I can't see why you like that awkward fellah there. He's the dead spit of a mongrel.'

Stapleton threw down his battered hat and then planted his left foot on the crown.

'This is my final word,' he shouted almost in hysterics. 'Keep him and any two you like of the others. Three is all she can handle; if you keep the big fellah. Keep him and you'll thank me one day for doing you a good hand's turn. Keep him and many is the day you'll go on your knees and say a prayer; thanking me for this blessed word.'

As usual, Fleming suddenly turned away and said:

'All right, Joe. Get rid of the four.'

'Wait a minute, Jack,' Stapelton said eagerly. 'Let's tackle the others one by one and make a good pick.'

'Make your own pick,' Fleming shouted from a distance.

'You won't be sorry,' Stapleton cried out happily in his sing-song girlish voice. 'You'll never regret letting me keep the makings of a great champion.'

True enough, the ungainly pup began to grow like a mushroom. His spectacular gain in strength and size, however, was at the expense of his surviving brother and sister. Indeed, those two might just as well have been drowned with the other four; because the monster gave them hardly any opportunity at all to suck the nectar of life from their mother's teats. The mercilesss glutton pushed and tumbled them like skittles; as he hurried fore and aft and along his field of supply; from morning to night; almost draining the warm fluid from each faucet at a single gulp.

After three months, it was obvious that the puny couple would never become race-dogs of any merit whatsoever; in spite of their extremely noble breeding, by the famous Boranno out of Hunkadory.

'My curse on you, Joe Stapleton,' Fleming said to his kennel man one day. 'See what you have done to a valuable litter? I wouldn't get a pound note for either of those two dwarfs.'

'Never mind, Jack,' Stapleton said with a beatific smile. 'Never mind the little ones and pay attention to that cock o' the walk. You have a natural champion in that big fellah there. Will you look at that giant and stop whinging.'

'My curse on him, too,' said Fleming. 'He has nearly sucked the living heart out of my lovely bitch.'

The two half-starved youngsters were given away to village boys and the sole survivor was called Bohunk. That rugged and cumbersome name suited him admirably; because he lacked the graceful lines and bearing of his breed during adolescence. Pot-bellied and lumpy and swaying in his walk, he was more like a pig than a greyhound. No wonder! He spent his whole time eating; or looking for food.

Since Fleming kept a small hotel, together with a poultry and dairy farm, Bohunk's teeth were never short of employment during these days. A brilliant thief and mitcher, he took and devoured everything that came within his reach, hot or cold, dead or alive. In fact, young chicklets were his favourite delicacy. He would leap the fence of the poultry yard and gobble up several of the helpless creatures, while the mother hens flapped their wings and screamed. In the same way, he made sudden forays into the kitchen and made off with large chunks of meat. He even sneaked into the bar and drank stout that was left unguarded at a convenient level.

Yet he showed remarkable speed and power of manoeuvre when Joe Stapleton began to take him out on the mountain for training. Springing from the leash like a bullet, he killed his first hare after three smart turns that brought tears of joy to the kennel man's eyes. Later, while being taught to race at a local track, he showed equal skill and intelligence. Not only did he break quickly from the trap, at the very first time of asking, but he stayed close to the rails and cornered just as handily as a veteran.

After seeing a private trial in which Bohunk beat older opponents by a distance of ground, Fleming became almost as enthusiastic as his kennel man.

'Listen, Joe,' he said, 'We may have a dog, in this fellah here, that could put all the bookmakers in Dublin on the floor.'

Stapleton knew at once that his employer had a sordid scheme in mind and protested strongly.

'I'll curse you to my dying day, Jack.' he said, 'if you try any of your tricks on a champion like Bohunk.'

Fleming smiled and then tapped Stapleton's chest with his fist.

'Bear this in mind, Joe,' he said softly. 'I'm not in the racing game as a public benefactor. You've boasted so much and you've talked so much that my dog is known from one end of the country to the other; even before he has set foot on a public track.'

'I've said it and I'll say it again,' shouted Stapleton, 'that if you tamper with Bohunk...'

'You know very well that I never use dope,' said Fleming.

'There are other ways,' said Stapleton.

'Shut up, Joe,' Fleming retorted. 'Right now, I couldn't get even money to a lousy tenner about my dog and it's all your fault. What am I to do? Run him for fun?'

True enough, he was unable to 'draw blood' to any extent worth mentioning on the first four races won by his phenomenal puppy; since the well-informed book-makers offered untouchable odds on each occasion.

However, he found the solution to his problem in another puppy that was almost equally good and whose owner was a close friend. He made a deal with Frank Holden, a Dublin publican that was also a heavy and unscrupulous gambler.

On the day of the race, he brought Stapleton into his private office and said:

'You're not coming to Dublin with us tonight, because I know you wouldn't like to see Bohunk lose.'

'Is that so?' Stapleton said gently.

'That's how it is, Joe,' Fleming said, as he threw four notes on the table. 'Take that score and have a good skite. You need one badly. For the past month, blast it, you've been going around like a hen with three eggs in her gut.'

Stapleton looked at the four new five-pound notes in silence for a few moments. Then he sighed and put them in his pocket.

'I know what you're going to do, Jack,' he said. 'Have it your own way. I'll be gone when you get back tonight.'

Worried by the lean man's gentle tone, Fleming laughed nervously.

'Don't go far,' he said. 'I want to see you in the morning. You'll get double your usual share of the win this time.'

As he walked to the door, Stapleton shook his head and muttered:

'I wouldn't touch a penny of that money, Jack. I'm going for good.'

Fleming struck the table in rage.

'I've heard that before,' he shouted.

At the door, Stapleton halted and looked back over his shoulder.

'You don't understand a great dog like Bohunk,' he said. 'You may run him off his feet beforehand, but he'll accept the challenge all the same when the time comes. He will, indeed. He'll race and maybe break his heart trying to win. Good bye now, Jack.'

Fleming struck the table again after the lean man had gone.

'My curse on that fool,' he growled.

As he drove to Dublin that evening in a closed van, together with Bohunk and his five punters, the foolish and hot-tempered fellow was still violently angry with Stapleton. Otherwise, he would not have made the unfortunate animal gallop so far on a lonely stretch of the wild mountain road.

'Let him run a bit farther,' he shouted in answer to the warnings and appeals for mercy of his henchmen. 'I want to make sure of my money. Bohunk 'll answer no challenge tonight.'

In fact, he refused to stop the car until his dog had begun to stagger from exhaustion. Immediately afterwards, however, he fondled and massaged the bewildered creature like a loving mother. Even so, Bohunk was still stretched out flat on his side, with his limp red tongue trailing along the floor of the van, when they reached the outskirts of the city.

After halting near a bus stop, Fleming gave each of his punters six hundred pounds. One third of that amount belonged to Holden.

'You all know what to do?' he asked.

They nodded.

'Just take up position when betting opens on the race and then wait for the signal. I'll be in my usual place. Run along now, lads. Go up there separately and don't talk to one another on the spot or to anybody else.'

He himself drove to the track and delivered Bohunk to the staff. By then, the huge fawn dog was able to walk at his normal lazy and twisting gait.

'By ganeys!' one of the attendants said. 'The terror of the Wicklow Hills looks stripped and ready for action tonight.'

'I sharpened him a bit,' Fleming said gruffly. 'He might scale a pound or two less.'

Then he hid in a neighbouring tavern and drank glass after glass of neat whiskey rapidly; as he always did while waiting for a heavy bet to reach the supreme moment of decision. His eyes were bloodshot and his heart-beat had become ominously irregular, as he climbed to the top of the stand through a dense crowd, a few minutes before the race.

Glancing furtively at the six dogs that were being led slowly round the track by white-smocked attendants. he noted with pleasure that Bohunk looked supine and indifferent.

'He won't run a yard,' big Jack muttered happily.

In spite of his dull appeareance, however, the fawn monster was a hot favourite in the ring; while Holden's dog was freely quoted at nine to two.

'Nine thousand for myself,' Fleming reflected greedily. 'If the lads manage to unload it all before the price shortens.'

He waited until the runners were being examined in front of the stand and then raised his hat casually. His men rushed in at once and began to bet. The wild flurry of excitement that ensued, all along the line of book-makers, was too painful to watch. With his eyes closed, he stood rigid and thoughtless until a sudden silence fell. Then he opened his eyes once more; as the dummy began to rumble round the track; while the enclosed dogs scratched and whined excitedly.

The crowd roared as the trap doors shot up and the dogs emerged.

'Come on, Bohunk.'

Fleming smiled as Holden's black dog, Bold Fenian, broke smartly and took the lead at once; while Bohunk trailed badly.

'It's in the bag,' he said aloud.

Nevertheless, Stapleton proved to have been right. Going down the back stretch, the fawn monster found an untapped reserve of strength in his gallant heart and began to race with a tremendous burst of speed that brought a wild shout of joy from the spectators.

'God Almighty!' Fleming muttered in horror.

Bohunk maintained his effort until he had overtaken and passed Bold Fenian right on the finish line. Then he collasped and had to be carried from the track by an attendant; while his triumphant backers cheered in ecstasy.

'God almighty!' Fleming kept repeating, as he staggered down from the stand with his head bowed.

On reaching home with his prostrate dog, he found that Stapleton had gone to London. By then, however, Fleming had drunk himself into a maudlin state and felt indifferent to his heavy loss. In fact, he had already begun to brood over a vision of golden and never-ending gain; the dazzling mirage that leads every gambler to perdition.

'What do I care about Stapleton?' he shouted. 'Let him stay away for ever if he wants. Neither do I give a straw for the two thousand that I lost. I care less about making Frank Holden an enemy for life. I have an unbeatable champion in my kennels; a gold mine on four legs if there ever was one. So why should I care? From here to Glasgow, you couldn't find a dog to take the sway from Bohunk. At first, I thought he was just a smart pup; same as you often see; a bright flash in the pan that is quenched by the first breath of powerful opposition. Now I'm certain that he's a real champion.'

True enough, Bohunk recovered within a month and

showed no sign of having been soured by his painful experience. Then he was taken by his foolish owner to the kennels of a famous trainer in Manchester. There he was caged and exercised and nourished according to a strict regime; instead of being allowed to roam and plunder at will, as he used to do under the wise rule of Joe Stapleton. So that the poor animal pined in his heart for the freedom of his native hills and for the gargantuan meals that he needed to maintain the power of his huge frame.

After he had finished dead last in five successive races, the trainer advised Fleming to take him home and turn him loose.

'In my opinion, Jack' Masterson said, 'only time will tell whether he can ever win again. It's always the case when a good young dog has been asked too much and too soon. He has taken a dislike to the game.'

For a fortnight after his return, Bohunk appeared to be the most content dog on earth, scavenging and roaming the hills from morning to night. Then he suddenly disappeared, leaving no trace.

'Let him go,' Fleming shouted on hearing the news. 'Thanks be to God that I'm rid of that monster at last. He has me ruined. He won when I backed him to lose. Then he lost, five solid times, one after the other, when I had him backed to win, right down to his paws. Five solid times! Not only has he got me on the floor, but I'll soon be boring underground like a mole. So I thank God that he's gone and let nobody look to see where he went. Now, may be, my luck is finally going to turn.'

Instead of turning, however, his luck got worse and worse. Six months later, his heart collapsed and he was taken to a nursing home in Dublin.

'Tell me the truth,' he said to the doctor after being examined. 'Am I going to be scratched from all engagements? Or am I still there with an outsider's chance?'

'Your only chance,' the doctor said, 'is to give up drink and...'

'Say no more,' Fleming said.

'I must,' said the doctor. 'If you go on betting. . . '

'Not another word,' Fleming insisted. 'I'd rather die right now than live without being able to bet.'

Depressed by that horrid prospect, he made no improvement until Joe Stapleton came into his room one day without warning. On catching sight of the kennel man, his boozy face contorted and his huge hands clutched the bedclothes in an access of delight. Even so, he pretended to be angry.

'It took you a long time to come,' he shouted. 'A false friend is the worst thing a man can have.'

'Take it easy now, Jack,' Stapleton whispered, approaching the bed on tip-toe. 'Take it easy like a good man I came as soon as possible.'

'Here I am,' Fleming continued, 'lying flat on my back for the past five weeks and you never sent a word.'

'Be quiet now, Jack,' Stapleton said gently, as he went on one knee by the bedside. 'It was how I didn't want to come empty-handed. Now, though, I have news that will get you out of here in two shakes of a lamb's tail.'

Fleming stared at Stapleton's exalted face and frowned. 'What mischief are you up to now?' he grumbled.

'Stop talking and listen quietly,' Stapleton whispered, 'because I have the news that you need.'

'What news?' said Fleming.

Stapleton took off his hat and then struck the crown a mighty blow with his left fist; as if it were a deadly enemy.

'Pat Harris kept writing,' he said, naming one of big Jack's punters, 'all the time I was working at Nick Dempsey's place in London. So I knew what was happening. I nearly got a fit when he told me that Bohunk had disappeared.'

'My curse on that dog,' Fleming said. 'He got me down.'

Stapleton struck the floor with his hat and continued:

'Feeling certain that he had been stolen, I kept making enquiries by letter among my friends; up and down the country. I had no luck at all, however, until the day before you were taken to this nursing home. Then Tom McCarthy brought four dogs over from Killarney to be trained by Nick Dempsey for the London tracks. While we were having a drink together that night, he told me about having seen a great fight at a small town near his own place three weeks previously. He said it was on account of a big fawn greyhound that a wandering tribe of Wicklow tinkers had trained to limp.'

Fleming sat up in bed and shouted in a rage:

'Are you crazy? How could they teach him to limp?'

'I'm only telling you what the man said,' Stapleton whispered.

'Then your friend McCarthy must be the king of liars,' Fleming insisted in the same tone. 'Sure it's well known that a greyhound has no brain. You couldn't train him to limp and more is the pity; or to anything else of the kind. God Almighty! A greyhound hasn't even got the sense of smell of a proper dog. All he has, blast him, is the keenest sight on earth and a great power of speed.'

'It was in a big field where races were held after Mass on Sunday,' Stapleton went on imperturbably, 'that McCarthy saw the fight. "Jakers," he said. "The battle of Clontarf was a tea party in comparison." A straight course of about two hundred yards was all those country people had. They used the motor of an old Ford car to work the dummy along a rail they stole somewhere and the rest of the gear as well. The strange fawn dog limped so badly on his way to the traps that everybody jeered and laughed at his chance. So the tinkers were able to get long odds for their money.'

The kennel man struck the crown of his hat a fierce blow and his girlish voice rose to its highest as he continued:

'Faith, there was nothing wrong with the big fawn greyhound when the race started. His four legs took him along like the wind and he won with the greatest of ease. Then he began to favour the right hind leg once more. Thereupon, the whole crowd of local people went stone mad. "The robbers have trained him to limp on purpose," they shouted. By the hammers of hell! Skin and hair were flying in all directions before you could make the sign of the Cross. According to McCarthy, those tinkers would have been lynched to a man only for the Civic Guards arrived in the nick of time. All the same, the hardy roadmen gave as much as they took and more power to their elbows. They got paid their bets into the bargain and drove out of town like conquering heroes with their lame dog.'

Fleming slid back down under the clothes and glared at the kennel man with hatred in his bleary eyes.

'Lame?' he muttered in a despondent tone. 'Was he really lame?'

'Of course, the poor creature was lame,' Stapleton said with a wise smile, as he got to his feet slowly. 'The tinkers didn't have to teach him anything. As soon as he caught sight of the dummy...'

'My curse on you, Joe Stapelton,' Fleming said bitterly.

'When the race started,' Stapleton continued, as he walked to the door on tip-toe, 'his great courage made him forget the lameness and he took up the challenge.'

'A lame dog?' Fleming shouted in a frenzy, as the kennel man opened the door. 'Is that the great news you brought?'

Stapleton thrust his head through the doorway and said:

'Bring him along now, Pat.'

Then Bohunk was led into the room by Pat Harris; a tall young man with a freckled face and curly red hair that protruded in a luxuriant cluster from the upward-slanting peak of his grey tweed cap.

'That monster!' Fleming cried out in horror. 'I might just as well stretch out and die before he can do me further harm.'

Stapleton raised the dog's right hind leg and said:

'See that paw, Jack? Two of the claws are missing. The tinkers found him caught in a trap they had set for rabbits, on the mountain above your place. They took him along and cured his foot. God bless them, but he'll always be lame.'

Then he unleashed Bohunk, who limped over to the hearth-rug and lay down at once.

'My curse on you, Joe Stapleton,' Fleming shouted. 'What good is a lame dog? Answer me, you fool.'

After glancing at his enraged owner with royal indifference, Bohunk stretched out with a deep sigh of content on the black rug.

'On hearing McCarthy's story,' Stapleton said, 'I travelled over to Kerry and followed the trail of those tinkers, up through Limerick and Clare into Galway. I heard they got into the same class of a fight at the fair of Ballinasloe. They were gone into Mayo, though, before I arrived. In the heel of the hunt, I had to follow them up hill and down dale, through Sligo and Leitrim and Monaghan, before running them to earth finally in the mountains of Louth. Then I sent for Pat Harris and he came with the van.'

Pat Harris wagged his head at Fleming and said:

'Lucky thing for Joe that I was there, boss. It would have gone hard with him, without a doubt, if he had tried to tackle those tinkers on his own hook. They were as tough as a body of men as you'd care to meet in fair play or foul. Although we had the documents and four Civic Guards, they put up a great fight before surrendering the dog.'

'Pity you didn't stay at home in that case,' Fleming said. 'I'd give a fair share of money never to see that monster again. What can I do with a lame dog? Even if he has regained his form, I wouldn't be allowed to run him at an official track.'

'That's true, Jack,' Stapleton whispered seductively, as he went on his knee once more by the bedside. 'He wouldn't be let run and even if he were, his limit is two hundred yards. The tinkers tried him over a longer distance and the poor creature...'

'My curse on you for a fool,' Fleming interrupted. 'You're a natural born twister and a fool.'

Stapleton hurled his battered hat into a corner of the room and then cried out in an exalted tone:

'The tinkers had a collie bitch in one of their caravans and she was nursing a litter of six. Every single one of those pups was the dead spit of Bohunk. Listen to me, Jack. Our champion had set his living mark on every one of that miserable mongrel's get. Am I right, Pat?'

Pat Harris wagged his head at Fleming and said:

'It's true, boss. I saw it with my own eyes; a litter of honest to God greyhound pups that came out of a collie. It was like a miracle.'

'As a sire,' Stapleton shouted in ecstasy, 'Bohunk 'll make your fortune and astonish humanity.'

The kennel man went on and on, extolling the pro-creative virtues of Bohunk, until Fleming got carried away once more by a vision of never-ending gain and triumphant satisfactions.

'What have I got to lose?' big Jack shouted at length.

Then Stapleton got to his feet and looked up at the ceiling with the fixed stare of a fanatic.

'I should have known from the start,' he whispered in rapture, 'that he was destined above all else to be the father of champions. Yet it was only when I saw that his royal seed had made princes and princesses of that miserable collie's pups...'

Fleming sat up in bed and yelled:

'Let's get going, lads. We have work to do. I'll mortgage my house and land to buy the best bitches in the country. Come on, Lads. Get me out of here fast.'

True enough, during the four years that he has been at stud, the fawn monster has paid generous tribute to Joe Stapleton's gift of prophecy; for the brilliance of his get has made Kilsallagh Kennels the richest and most famous in the land. Although still far from the goal set by his loyal protector, he seems quite capable of breeding a thousand champions before his death.

The public, of course, has given Fleming all the credit for Bohunk's lucrative triumphs as a sire. Yet it must be admitted that big Jack himself invariably contradicts the flatterers that crowd into his cromium-plated lounge bar; where he holds court every Sunday afternoon.

'Listen, you fellahs,' he shouts. 'I owe everything to Joe Stapleton including the fact that I can still drink and bet without danger to my health. Only for Joe, I'd have died bankrupt four years ago. He has the knack, blast him, whether it's a knack or a gift. Who cares what it is? He has it, in any case.'

A CROW FIGHT

*T*here were twenty crows' nests in an oak tree that overlooked a mountain road. There were young birds in all the nests. It was in the middle of May, and the tree was green with leaves. All day the old crows filled the air for a long distance with the raucous sound of their voices.

There was a nest built on a low branch some distance down from the other nests. So that the people who passed threw stones at it. Very many tourists passed that way going to the mountains, because the road led from Dublin to the mountains. One day a party of three young men were passing, and they threw stones. Two of the young men threw two stones apiece, and then wiped their hands in their handkerchiefs and went away. They said: 'Let's go on. That's hard work on a hot day like this.' But the third young man was an American tourist, and he said: 'No, by Golly, I'm going to stay until I show you fellahs how to knock down that nest.'

He gave a little peasant boy sixpence to collect stones for him. After throwing stones for an hour or so, the American put a small stone through the bottom of the nest, and it fell to the ground. The American laughed, and went away to the publichouse farther up the road, where his Irish friends had retired to wait for him. He took no notice of the small crow that had fallen to the ground with the nest. The peasant boy also went away at a run to buy sweets for his sixpence without taking any notice of the little crow.

The little crow had no feathers on his body. Things like soft fluffy bristles grew all over him. He had fallen in a clump of long grass by the roadside and he was quite unhurt. But he was very terrified. With his mouth open and his bare wings stretched out, he worked his neck from side to side as if he was trying to unscrew it from his body. The straw from the broken nest lay all around him on the green long grass and on the white limestone road.

The old crows had fled when the stone-throwing began. They watched the affair from a high tree one hundred yards away from the nesting tree. They had grown quite used to the stone-throwing, and they were not in the least annoyed. They 'cawed' and they sharpened their beaks while they waited. But when they saw the nest falling they raised a wild and prolonged and raucous 'caw'. They flapped their wings and made a movement as if they had suddenly become intoxicated and were falling off their perches.

The mother of the young crow that had fallen flew into the air and turned a somersault three times with rage and sorrow. It was more through rage than sorrow, because she was a very old crow, and things had been going badly with her for the past month. Her mate had run away with a young female crow and gone to nest in an ash tree on the other side of the hill beyond the torrent. Two of her young ones had died on the day they came out of their shells. They died through exposure, since she had to leave them uncovered while she sought food. And now the third and last one had fallen to the ground, and she was without a nest even.

She flew back to the nesting tree, uttering harsh cries.

She landed on the topmost branch and looked around.
There was nobody in sight. A rabbit had already run out
on to the road. He was looking about him, sitting on his
thighs with his ears cocked. The old mother crow
swooped down and landed in the middle of the road.
She thrust out her chest, blinked her eyes, reached out
her head sideways, listening. She 'cawed' gently. An
answering mumble came from the long grass by the
road-side where the young crow lay. The old mother
crow immediately darted over. When she saw the young
one, sprawled on its belly and with its distended mouth
raised in the habitual manner to receive food, the old
mother crow became overcome with emotion and she
broke out into a series of thunderous and melancholy
'caws'. She jumped and ran about the road and flapped
her wings like one gone mad.

The other crows gathered about. Some flitted on idle
wings. Others sat on the fences that bound the road on
either side. Now and again some would walk over
sedately, reach out their necks and peer at the young-
ster that had been unnested. There was a terrific din.

Then the old mother crow flew up into the tree and
darted about from branch to branch as if she were
seeking something. Then she flew back to the road.
She seized her young one in her beak and in her claws.
With a sudden swoop she arose and landed in the fork
of the lowest branch of the tree. The other crows
followed her, 'cawing,' urging her on as it were. She
rested for several minutes in the fork of the branch,
fondling the young one. The young crow was terrified
once more by the fresh experience, and it held its
mouth open, as if it were expecting something to attack
it.

Then the mother lifted it again in her claws and flew
upwards with a mighty effort. She landed on the second
branch from the top. There were four nests there,
made along the branch, supported by the twigs that

grew thickly on either side of the branch, like the prongs of a comb. She planted her young one in a nest where there were two young crows ready to fly away. She attacked the two young crows furiously with beak and claw and drove them out of the nest. Then she spread herself out over the young one and waited for the attack from the parents of the young crows that she had expelled. The two young crows that had been expelled spread their wings and tried to soar. But their bodies were yet too heavy for their wings, and instead of rising they fell slantwise and landed clumsily on their breasts in the field, about one hundred yards away. There they lay, panting.

The two old crows rose screaming. They attacked the old mother crow with all their might. They showered blows on her back and head. They rooted at her with their claws and sent black feathers flying from her scratched back. She fought them as best she could in return. But principally she clung with all her might to the nest, determined to die rather than be ejected or expose her young one to death. The other crows gathered about the fighting ones. There was a terrific din.

The fight lasted fully a quarter of an hour, and then it stopped. The old mother crow was battered, but she still remained on the nest. The other two crows suddenly flew away to the field where their young ones had landed. For some time they strutted about 'cawing' to their young ones, sharpening their beaks and flapping their wings and making growling noises as if they threatened to go back again to the mother crow.

But they obviously thought better of it. Instead they set to teaching their young ones how to scratch the earth and drag out worms without cutting them with their beaks, and thus losing the better part of them.

KING OF INISHCAM

Iwas Superintendant of Police in the district
of Kilmorris. It is one of the most remote
parts of Ireland, on the west coast. The inhabitants are all practically of pure Gaelic
stock, and during the centuries of English occupation they retained most of their old
customs. A very fine race of men, industrious, thrifty,
extremely religious, and proud to a fanatical degree.
To illustrate this latter characteristic the case of Sean
McKelvey seems to me worthy of record.

He lived on the small island of Inishcam, which is
separated from the mainland by a narrow channel of
about a quarter of a mile. Even so, this tiny channel
renders the island an excellent headquarters for its
principal industry, which is, or was at least, the distilling of illicit whiskey, We call it poitheen locally.

Except for one narrow cove, the island is surrounded
by rugged cliffs, so it was an easy matter for scouts
to give warning when any of my men came from the
mainland to search for the still. And the islanders went
on merrily distilling for the first year of my service
in the district, just as they had been doing for centuries.
In the same way, when the spirits were ready for the
market, they could sneak over during the night in

their currachs to the mainland and dispose of their goods in safety. I was at my wits' end as to how to deal with the nuisance.

Ours is a democratic police force, and, as I understand it, the business of a good police officer is to preserve order in his district at the expense of as little coercion as possible. It was impossible to adopt rough measures with the twenty-five or thirty families on the island. There would be a rumpus on the mainland, followed by the usual protests to Dublin by people who are always looking for a chance to accuse the police force of tyrannical conduct. I decided that the only thing to do was to tackle Sean McKelvey in person.

He was the chief man on Inishcam and was commonly called The King, a title which is claimed by some romantic people to have come from ancient times, before Gaelic civilization was overthrown by the British, but whose origin is really quite recent and rather ridiculous, as is usually the case with most of these titles of nobility. Sometime during the eighties of last century, a party of British military and police invaded the island in the hope of being able to collect some rent from the inhabitants, who had paid none for years. On the approach of the authorities, the inhabitants fled to the cliffs, leaving only the aged and the infants in the village. The officer in charge picked on one dignified old fellow as the most likely to be able to give him information and assistance in dealing with the others.

'Are you the head man of this island?' he asked.

The old man bowed, understanding no English.

The officer told him to have his islanders parade at the rent office with their rent within one month, or else their property would be impounded. Then he went away, and some newspaper reporter picked on the incident for a story, and the story reached London, and presently there were scholars and other faddists coming to the island to visit the last remaining Irish King. In that way old McKelvey, Sean's grandfather, received the title, and his descendants inherited it, and the islanders politely accepted the situation, since it brought them revenue from summer visitors.

However, if a man is called King, even in fun, he develops a kingly manner in course of time. Sean McKelvey, being the third of this line of monarchs, was firmly convinced of his royal blood and behaved as if he had divine right to rule over Inishcam. Many a time he was heard to say on the mainland, when he came there on business, that the police had no authority over him and that, if they made any attempt to interfere with his person, he would die rather than submit to the indignity. And the islanders believed him. So that it can be easily understood it was a ticklish business putting an end to his distillery.

I dressed in civilian clothes and got a man to row me over to the island, on which I landed alone and unarmed, to beard The King in his realm.

It was a fine summer morning, and, when I jumped ashore on the little sandy beach, I saw a crowd of the islanders lounging on a broad, flat rock near the village, which stands above the beach. I climbed the steep, rocky path, which was like the approach to a fortress. They all stared at me as I came to the rock, but nobody spoke. They knew who I was and were not pleased to see me.

I will admit that I grew slightly uneasy, for the men on that island are of tremendous physique, tall, slim, and as hard as whipcord. The surroundings were even more menacing than the islanders themselves. Beyond the village, there was some arable lands, covered with patches of rye and potatoes. Beyond that rose the mountains, covered with heather and cut by deep, gloomy valleys. Fat chance my men would have trying to find a still in that impassible wilderness.

'Good morning, men,' I said cheerfully. 'I have come to see The King.'

A man nodded over his shoulder towards a house in the center of the village. It was a one-storied cottage like the rest, with a slate roof, but it was longer, and its walls had a pink wash, whereas the others were whitewashed. Some flowers grew in the yard in front of it, beside a heap of lobster pots and nets that were hanging up to dry.

I strode towards the house. When I entered the yard, a man appeared in the doorway with his arms folded on his bosom. It was Sean McKelvey, The King of the island.

'You want to see me?' he said arrogantly.

He was about six feet in height and as straight as a rod. He was dressed only in his shirt and trousers, which were fastened at the waist by a red handkerchief. His shirt was open at the neck, and the sleeves were rolled up beyond his biceps, which were stiff, owing to his arms being folded. He was as muscular as a prize fighter in training, and as I glanced at his muscles I doubted the good sense of my plan. There was a fair stubble on his powerful jaws and upper lip, increasing the menacing expression of his arrogant countenance. His blue eyes seemed to bore through me, as they say in romances. In fact, he looked every inch a King, and I wished that he had chosen somebody else's district for his damned distilling, for his type is one I admire. But the law is th law and must be upheld.

'Yes,' I answered. 'I've come to see you, McKelvey.'

'As friend or foe?' he cried.

Affecting a calm which I did not feel, I took a cigarette from my case and tapped the end on the lid. The other men began to crowd around the yard.

'Whichever way you like to take it, ' I said.

'Well! That means you've come as an enemy,' said McKelvey.

'I suppose you know who I am,' I said.

'Troth, then I do,' said he. 'I know who ye are well enough but I don't give a toss rap for you or yer men. You have nothing against me. So I don't want you nosing about this island.'

'Oh! Yes, I have something against you, McKelvey.'

'What is it?'

'You make poitheen here.'

'I'm not saying that we do, but even if we do it has nothing to do with you.'

'I'm afraid it has. I am police officer of this district and I won't have you or anybody else poisoning the people with your rotten drink. That's what I came to see you about.'

'Well! You have your journey for nothing. I'm taking no orders from you, Mr Corrigan.'

'I'm not giving you orders but if you had the courage of a man I'd like to make a bargain with you.'

His face darkened, and he leaned back slightly as if he were going to spring at me. He unfolded his arms, and his hands crept slowly down by his sides, the fingers doubling over the palms.

'What's that I heard you saying?' he whispered.

He came forward two paces slowly, just like an animal getting into position for a pounce. Even at that moment I had to admire the magnificent stance of the man. The other islanders behind me began to growl, and I knew that my bait had taken.

'If you had the courage of a man,' I repeated in a low, offensive sort of tone, 'I'd like to make a bargain with you.'

'And what makes you think,' drawled McKelvey, 'that I haven't the courage of a man?'

At that moment a young woman appeared in the doorway with a baby in her arms. She was a handsome woman with red hair, with a rather startled expression in her eyes.

'Sean,' she cried, 'What ails you?'

He wheeled around like a shot and barked at her: 'Go into the house, Mary.'

She obeyed instantly, and he turned back to face me.

'Speak what's in your mind,' he cried.

'It's like this, McKelvey,' I said casually. 'You and your still are a damn nuisance in my district. You call yourself King of this island, and I'm the local police officer, whose business it is to see that the law is observed. There isn't room for the two of us. Well! This is what I propose. I'm ready to fight you and let the winner have the sway. If you win you can carry on with your still, and I give you my word of honour that I'll not interfere with you in future. If I win, you'll come along with me to the police barracks and give a written guarantee that you'll break up your still and obey the law in future. How does that strike you as a fair deal? I'm putting it to you as man to man. If you have the guts of a man you'll agree to it.'

For a few moments there was dead silence. The infant began to cry within the house. And then McKelvey sighed deeply, swelled out his chest, nodded. I noticed that the whites of his eyes had gone red and the veins on his neck stood out, as if they were going to burst with outraged anger.

'So help me God,' he muttered, 'I'm going to kill you for this if I have to swing for it.'

'Just a moment,' I said. 'I have come here alone. Are you going to give me fair play and are you going to agree to the bargain I proposed?'

I wanted to infuriate him as much as possible in order to give myself a better chance of beating him.

'Who the hell do ye think yer dealing with?' he roared. 'A rat like yourself or Sean McKelvey, the King of Inishcam?'

'Then it's a bargain,' I said.

'Put up your fists,' he roared.

'Give me time to strip,' I said, unbuttoning my coat.

As I took off my coat and waistcoat leisurely, he stood in front of me, shaking with anger and then he suddenly seemed to collect himself and to master his rage. He bit his lip, and a queer, startled look came into his eyes. For all the world, he looked at that moment like a wild animal of the African forest confronted by a hunter for the first time, awed and at the same time infuriated. He stooped down and slipped off his shoes. Then he pulled his socks up over the ends of his trouser legs and rubbed some sand from the yard on his palms. By that time I was set for action.

'I'm ready now if you are,' I said.

'Then take your medicine,' he hissed.

With that he drove with his right at my chin, and I ducked just in time to let it graze the right side of my head. Even so, it rocked me to my heels and it enabled me to judge the calibre of the man with whom I had to deal. I realized that my only chance was in being able to avoid the sledge hammer that he carried in his right hand, until his frenzy exhausted him. Ducking and skipping about the yard, I kept teasing him in order to keep his rage at fever pitch.

'So you think you can fight, do you, McKelvey?' I sneered. 'You couldn't hit a haystack. I'm ashamed to fight you. It's like taking milk from a child. You'd better surrender before I do you damage. What's the use? Look at that. You thought it was my head and it was only the air. Man alive, who told you you could fight?.

And sure enough, although he had the strength and agility of a tiger, he was handicapped by knowing nothing about boxing. All he could do was to swing that terrifying right hand and trust to luck. Little by little he began to tire, and I was overjoyed to hear that tell-tale panting.

'Now for it,' I thought.

I waded into him and landed twice on his chin with all the power in my body behind each blow, but the only result was that I smashed two knuckles in my left hand. McKelvey swayed backwards and then for the first time swung his left hand wildly and met me straight on the chest. I went back four yards before I fell, all in a heap, conscious but at the same time convinced that my ribs had been smashed to splinters and that the breath had been driven from my body. A great roar went up from the islanders.

I turned over and waited on my hands and knees until I recovered a little and then struggled to my feet. Had McKelvey gone for me at once it would have been his show, but the fool was dancing around the yard like a wild Indian, boasting of his prowess.

'There's not a man in Ireland that I wouldn't do the same to,' he yelled. 'Aye, or ten men either. I'll take every peeler they have and break every bone in their bodies. I'm Sean McKelvey, King of Inishcam, and I dare them to lay a hand on me.' And then he gave a wild yell that re-echoed through the mountains.

His men yelled in response, and somehow that pulled me together.

'Hold on there,' I said. 'You're not done with me yet, you windbag. Come and take it.'

Crouching, he came towards me, his underlip turned downwards.

'Is it more ye want, ye rat?' he muttered. 'Very well, then. Take that.'

Taking his time and no doubt thinking that, because I slouched and swayed a bit, I was easy prey, he swung his right at me once more. It was so slow coming that I could have countered it. In the meantime I dived in and landed a beauty on the mark. He grunted and doubled up. Then I lashed out with a vengeance, having found his tender spot.

'Don't kill him,' screamed his wife, running out into the yard.

The child wailed in the house, and several women. who had gathered to see the fight, also began to scream. The men, however, standing in a sullen group, were silent and astonished. In every one of their faces I saw a look of utter astonishment, as I glanced around at them nervously, not at all certain that they were not going to fall on me for having dishonoured their king. Not a bit of it. They stood there gaping, obviously unable to understand how it had come to pass that their invincible chief was down in a heap on the ground.

By the time I had finished dressing, McKelvey had come to his senses. He got to his feet and looked at me with an expression I shall never forget. It was an expression of bitter hatred, and at the same time there was in his eyes the picture of a shame that had already eaten to his very soul. At that moment I wished from the bottom of my heart that the result had been different. I saw that I had mortally wounded the poor man.

'You took me unawares,' he said quietly. 'It wouldn't happen again in a thousand years, if we met hand to hand every day of that thousand years. I lost my temper. You are a cunning man. Now what do you want with me? You won. I'm not able to go on with it.'

And his strange, wild, blue eyes were fixed on mine, boring through me. Damn it! Never in my life have I felt more ashamed and sorry than at that moment.

'You'll have to surrender your still, McKelvey,' I said, 'and come with me just as you promised.'

He lowered his eyes to the ground and answered: 'I'll do that. Come on with me into the house.'

Then indeed a strange thing happened. When I had followed him into the house, he went down to the hearth, where a small fire was burning. He took a heather broom from a corner of the hearth and began to sweep ashes over the burning embers.

'What are you doing, Sean?' said his wife, who stood nearby with the infant.

He did not answer but continued to sweep the ashes over the embers until he had extinquished the flames and there was no more smoke coming from the pile. Then he dropped the broom and stood erect.

'Come now into the garden,' he said.

I followed him out through the back door into the garden that adjoined the house. There he handed me a pinch of earth and a twig which he tore from a briar bush, the ancient formula for surrendering legal possession of his house and grounds.

'But you can't do this,' I said.

He drew himself up and answered arrogantly: 'You won. You are now the master. Isn't that what you wanted to be?'

'But I only want your still. I don't want your house and land. Man alive, are you mad?'

'You'll get the still as well,' he said. 'You're not thinking I'd go back on me word?'

He beckoned me to follow him, and I did.

He was still in his stockinged feet and he moved as nimbly as a goat over the rough ground, leaping from rock to rock, at a brisk trot, so that I had great difficulty in keeping up with him. We circled a spur of the mountain that rose immediately behind the village and then climbed from ledge to ledge along a precipitous path that brought my heart to my mouth, until finally we arrived in a ravine. About midway down the ravine, he turned suddenly to the left and when I reached him he was pulling loose rocks away from what proved to be the mouth of a cave. We entered the cave and moved in almost complete darkness along a narrow passage between two smooth walls, against which my shoulders brushed when I stumbled over the loose granite slivers that covered the floor.

I was now in an extremely nervous state. Has he brought me here to kill me? I wondered.

The thought was a natural one. For a man in his state, his pride deeply humbled at being knocked down in the presence of his people and then going through the ceremony of 'sod and twig' to kill his conqueror in an access of frenzy would be the most likely thing in the world. I remembered his terrible eyes and the unnatural calm of his bearing since he had risen after his fall.

At last I could not prevent myself from crying out to him, in a voice which must have disclosed the fear that was upon me, 'Where are you taking me, McKelvey?'

'We're nearly there,' he said quietly.

And then my fear vanished, and I felt ashamed of having suspected him.

Presently the cave grew lighter, and then we emerged from the narrow walls suddenly into an open space overlooking the sea. Here, to my astonishment, I found the distillery in full blast, attended by three men who looked at us in speechless astonishment. The still was set up in a natural chamber formed by an overhanging brow of the granite cliff, and there were kegs of the finished product stacked in a corner.

'Give your orders.' said McKelvey.

One of the men began to speak rapidly to McKelvey in Irish, using the dialect of the island which I did not understand, although I have a passable knowledge of the language. McKelvey answered the man with some heat, and then the two other men joined in the argument, until it ceased all of a sudden on a shout from McKelvey. Then again he turned to me.

'Give your orders,' he said.

'Well!' I said. 'I suppose the easiest way is to chuck them over the cliff. The rocks below will do the rest.'

'Very well,' he said.

He turned to the men and gave them orders in Irish.

They proceeded to obey him with great reluctance. I stood until the last of the stuff had been dragged to the edge and hurled down the steep face of the cliff, to smash on the rocks four hundred feet below.

'That's that,' I said. 'Now, let's go.'

Not a word was spoken until we got back to the village. There I noticed that the whole population was gathered on the flat rock, talking excitedly in low voices. By the way they looked at us as we approached I knew that McKelvey's reign was at an end.

I waited outside in the yard while he went indoors to dress. Then he appeared again, in his best clothes.

'Are you ready?' I said.

'If it's all the same to you,' he said, 'I won't go with you but I'll follow you.'

'But why not come with me?' I said. 'I have a boat down here, and it can bring you back again.'

'Well!' he said. 'I swore that I'd never be taken to a police barracks or before a magistrate alive.'

'But this is not a case of going to a police barracks or a magistrate. This is a personal thing between you and myself. It has nothing to do with the law.'

'All the same,' he said, 'the people wouldn't understand that. If I went with you now they'd say you took me prisoner.'

I stared at him in astonishment. How could it be possible that he could still stand on ceremony, after having made such a complete surrender? Now that he was dressed and in spite of the stubble on his cheeks, he looked more a king that ever, and nobody would believe that it was the same man who had danced around like a wild Indian after having felled me. He looked so austere and dignified and magnificently handsome. But his eyes had lost their arrogance, and they had the bitter expression of a defeated man. There was no hatred in his eyes, but they gave the harrowing picture of a sorrow that could not be cured.

'I understand that,' I said. 'Then I have your word for it that you'll come along later.'

'I give you my word,' he said proudly.

I hurried away, anxious to get out of sight of those eyes. When I reached the office and told Sergeant Kelly what had happened he could hardly believe me.

'Just you wait,' I said. 'McKelvey will be here himself shortly.'

'He'll never come,' said Kelly. 'The man would rather eat his own children than put a foot in this office,'

'We'll see,' I said.

And true enough, about an hour later, McKelvey marched in to the office.

In the meantime I had drawn up a document, which he signed without reading it. It was all very irregular but it was the only way I could deal with a difficult situation. After all, fine character and all that he was, he was a public menace, and I had to put a stop to his distilling some way or other.

'Is that all you want of me now, Mr Corrigan?' he asked when he had finished.

'No,' I said. 'I'd like to shake hands with the finest man I ever met.'

He looked at my outstretched hand and then looked me straight in the eyes and shook his head.

'Oh! Come on, man,' I said. 'Let's be friends. One of us had to win. I've taken a licking myself many a time and I dare say I'll take a good many more. Don't hold it against me. I was only trying to do my duty as best I could. After all, you were breaking the law, and I had to stop you.'

'I wasn't breaking my own law,' he said quietly.

And with that he marched out of the room with his head in the air.

'Keep an eye on him, Kelly,' I said to the sergeant.

I had an idea that he might begin to drink at one

of the local public houses and then run amuck before returning to his island. From past experience I knew that men of his type are extremely dangerous, once they lose their self-control with drink.

However, McKelvey did nothing of the kind. He marched down to the shore, staring straight in front of him and rowed back to the island without speaking to a soul.

'Well! That's that,' I said to the sergeant. 'McKelvey'll give us no more trouble with his still.'

'I hope not,' said Kelly, 'but I have me doubts.'

My own doubts were of a somewhat different kind. I was afraid that I had done the man a mortal injury and many a time during the following week I cursed the fate that had destined me to be a police officer and one with a conscience at that. Had the man been a mean and treacherous scoundrel I should have had no compunction about overthrowing him by means of a rather doubtful trick. But he was, on the contrary, a splendid type that is of immense value to any community.

On the ninth day afterwards his wife called at my hotel while I was having lunch. I went out to see her. She looked ill and terribly worried. She had obviously been weeping quite recently.'

I'm Mrs. McKelvey from Inishcam,' she said. 'I came to see you about my husband.'

'You look ill,' I said. 'Won't you sit down? Could I get you a drink of some sort?'

'No, Mr Corrigan,' she said gently, 'it's nothing like that I want. But wouldn't you come over and do something for Sean? He's been terrible since that day you came to the island, and I'm greatly afraid that he'll never rise again from his bed unless you can stop the people from thinking he was taken.'

'How do you mean?' I said.

'Well! It's how the people said that you took him,

which you know well, Sir, is a lie. And it broke his heart that they should say that about him. He took to his bed and he won't take bite or sup. He'll die that way. I know he will, for he's that proud.'

That was just what I feared, I told her to return at once to her home and that I would come over early in the afternoon.

'For God's sake, Sir,' she said, 'don't let him know that I came to see you. That would kill him altogether.'

'Don't be afraid, Mrs. McKelvey,' I said. 'I'll see to that.'

After she had gone, I did some hard thinking and finally hit upon a plan which, I felt sure, would succeed with the type of man that McKelvey was. This time I crossed over to the island in uniform, in accordance with the idea I had in mind. There were some people down on the beach, taking a catch of fish from the currachs that had just landed. I noticed that they touched their hats to me and bid me good day, quite unlike their conduct on my previous visit, when they scowled at me in silence. Presumably they had transferred their allegiance to the man who had defeated their King. Human nature is an odd business. Most of them followed me up to McKelvey's house and stood around the yard when I entered.

'God save all here,' I said.

'You too, Sir,' said Mrs. McKelvey, who was alone in the kitchen.

As she spoke she put her fingers to her lips, as a sign that I was to say nothing about her visit to my hotel.

I nodded and inquired: 'Is Mr. McKelvey at home?'

'He's in the room, Sir, in bed,' she said. 'Won't you go in?'

I thanked her and entered the bedroom, where I found McKelvey lying on his back in the bed, his arms folded on his bosom, his head propped up high by pillows. His face was very pale, and his eyes looked sunken. I strode over to the bed, and angry scowl on my face.

'So this is your idea of keeping your word, McKelvey,' I said with a sneer. 'What the devil do you mean by it? Are you making fun of me?'

I spoke as loudly as possible, so that the islanders outside could hear. McKelvey did not move for some moments. Then he sat bolt upright in bed and the colour came back to his pale cheeks. His eyes flashed with their old fire. He roared at his wife.

'Give me my clothes, Mary,' he cried. 'Leave the room, you. I'll talk to you on my feet and I'll talk to you outside my door for I'll not commit murder on my hearth.'

I left the house and waited while he dressed. I could hear the people murmuring behind me in the yard and wondered what was going to be the outcome of infuriating this man, who was very likely by now out of his senses. However, as he came towards me, tightening his red handkerchief around his waist, dressed exactly as he had been the day I fought him, I could see that he was in his proper senses.

'Now you can say what you have to say,' he cried. 'And this time, I'm warning ye, it's going to be a fight to the finish.'

'I don't want to fight you, McKelvey,' I said. 'This time I have come here as a police officer to make a complaint, and it's this. Nine days ago you came to my office of your own free will and gave a guarantee, as King of this island of Inishcam, that you were going to prevent your islanders, from manufacturing spirits and selling them illegally on the mainland, which is my territory. Is that true or is it not? Is it true that you came voluntarily to my office and gave me that guarantee?'

He stared at me and then he said in a loud voice: 'It is true.'

'It is also true that you are King of this island, is it

not?'

'It is true,' he cried in a still louder voice.

'Well! Then, why don't you act up to your promise?'

'In what way have I broken it?' he cried furiously.

'I have received information that one of your men has been to the mainland within the last few days, trying to buy another still to replace the one we threw over the cliff.'

I had, of course, received no such information but I had a shrewd idea that something of the kind might have been on foot. In any case, it had the desired effect.

McKelvey thrust out his chest and cried: 'There may have been one of my men on the mainland looking for a still, but if he lands with it on this island I'll break every bone in his body. I've been sick for the past week but from now on I'm on my feet, and you may take your gospel oath that what I say I'll do will be done.'

'Well! In that case,' I said in a humble tone, 'I'm very sorry to have spoken so roughly, Mr McKelvey. I apologize. I can only beg your pardon.'

'You have it and welcome, Mr. Corrigan,' he said, his face beaming with a great joy. 'And now, sir, I'm going to take that hand I refused to take before, if ye do me the honour.'

We shook hands, and I do believe that I never have felt so happy in my life as when I grasped the hand of that magnificent man. Nor did I ever afterwards, during my service in the district, have the least trouble with poitheen making on Inishcam.

TIMONEY'S ASS

On the little island of Finnbar there was an old fisherman called Timoney, who was always getting into trouble with the police. This was partly due to the fact that he smuggled illicit whiskey from the mainland and partly due to a black ass that he owned.

Timoney had no land, and so there was nowhere the ass could graze except on the yard before his master's cottage or along the roadside. In the rocky yard there was no vegetation other than a few briars and nettles that sprouted from beneath the fence. They did not sprout to any great extent, because the hungry ass pounced on the buds before they hardly had time to draw their first nourishment from the sun's rays. The roadside, on the other hand, was a paradise of lush grass. But alas! According to law, it was forbidden to trespass on the roadside. Any animal that devoured the rich grass was prosecuted.

During the fishing season, from April to November, the black ass led a life that was not entirely miserable. Timoney came to the chief village of Port Morogh every day from the hamlet of Clash, where he lived. He brought lobsters and other fish in the ass's creels. He sold the fish to the tourists and officials of the government who resided at Port Morogh. Inasmuch as Timoney was an old man and walked very slowly, the ass could pluck the grass as he ambled along. At the end of each journey, he had usually eaten his fill.

In winter it was a different story. It was then that Timoney made trips to the mainland in his little boat, returning with kegs of the fiery potheen. He buried the liquor in remote glens and then peddled it to the people secretly. Such was the man's cunning that the police were never able to catch him, and so they took revenge on his ass.

The poor animal had become just as cunning as his master, owing the the harsh necessities of his existence. He only grazed on the roadside at night, creeping along in the shadow of the fence, with his long ears cocked for the unheralded approach of his enemies. By daylight he could easily recognize their blue uniforms, and he took to flight when he caught sight of them. In the darkness of night, however, they were upon him many times before he became aware of their nearness. They would seize him and lead him to prison.

The prison for law-breaking animals was called the Pound. It was a tiny circular field at the back of the courthouse in the village of Port Morogh. The ground within this circular enclosure was as naked as a monk's skull, owing to the great number of animals that were constantly being imprisoned. It must be admitted that the people of Finnbar were grossly addicted to the vice of trespassing in those days. Their land was very poor, and yet they were entirely dependent on it for their meat and clothing. Therefore, grass was more precious to them than gold. They constantly drove their animals to graze on the share of their neighbours, who took revenge by taking the trespassers to the Pound. The owners of the impounded creatures then rushed to the police barracks, paid the fine demanded by law, and rescued their property.

The other animals were never impounded for more than a day, but Timoney's ass often remained a week within the enclosure. His master was in no hurry to rescue him. It must be confessed that the old man was by no means a reputable character. Far from feeling pity for the ass, Timoney would have left the animal in the Pound during the whole winter to die of hunger had he not been aware that the ass would again become necessary as a carrier in spring. Timoney also knew that the fine increased according to the length of imprisonment, and so he paid up within a week and then lashed the animal on the way home.

Then the people rose against the government and there was war on the mainland. The island of Finnbar was not affected by the revolt, yet the inhabitants benefitted by it, for the government was forced to withdraw its garrisons from isolated posts to concentrate on the business of holding the larger towns against the people's army. One day in early summer, a gunboat came from the mainland and took away all the officials. The police, the coastguardsmen, the magistrate, and even the process server all sailed away on a man-of-war. The islanders were left to their own devices for maintaining order.

This event was a great blessing for Timoney's ass. Not only did it free him from the men in blue uniforms, who took delight in dragging him to prison, but it also rid him of his cruel master. Timoney grieved bitterly over the evacuation, for he lost a market for his delicious lobsters. Furthermore, such is the contrariness of human nature, the people of Finnbar became extremely law-abiding as soon as the police left their territory, and led by their parish priest, they took proper measures against any further traffic among them in fiery spirits. In this manner, Timoney was deprived of both his markets, He was so mortally wounded in spirit by this dual calamity that he sickened and died.

Since he had no living relatives, nobody claimed his property. Thus, the black ass gained freedom by default.

At first, the fortunate animal was unaware of his freedom. When he went out to graze on the roadside at night, he kept his ears cocked as before, on watch for the approach of his enemies. In the morning, when he returned to his former master's yard, tremors passed along his scarred hide. But the door of his master's cabin remained closed, nobody came to put a halter on him, and on the roadside he met other animals grazing without apparent fear. Thus, with the passing of time, he grew bold.

The ass took to the roadside by daylight and grazed at will. His black hide filled out with an abundance of good flesh. The weals made by the lash disappeared, as well as the sores on his spine. In the old days, when Timoney was alive, the ass wore the neck-tether when not at work. This was a neck halter with two straps that were attached to the fetlocks of his forelegs, and which had brought his head down to within a few inches of the ground. Free of the halter now, and stimulated by a steady diet of good food, the ass gradually raised his head and arched his neck. By the time his winter coat had begun to sprout with the coming of the first cold winds from the ocean, the black ass that had once belonged to old Timoney, the fisherman, had gone wild.

One morning as he arose from his night's resting place in the yard of his former master, a fierce shower of hailstones struck the earth. They struck also at his hide with the force of sharp spurs. Their force and the wild harmony of the gale gave violent outlet to the new spirit that has grown in him with his change of circumstance. He stood for a few minutes with his ears pricked and his nostrils arched, braced against the hail. Then he snorted and began to trot about the yard, his unshod hoofs making dull thuds on the frosty ground. He went round and round the yard, gathering speed, until finally he broke into a gallop and opened wide his jaws to bray on a shrill note.

Suddenly he broke from his circuit and leaped through the gap in the fence where there had once been a wooden gate. He galloped up the lane and then along the highroad. He followed the highroad for some way, until he came to another lane that wound northward toward the mountainous summit of the island. The gale was coming from the south, where the ocean stretched without limit. Half carried by the force of the storm, he continued to gallop up the steep path that led northward to the mountain. And then the path ended. He was suddenly in a strange, uninhabited wilderness, He broke his gait, lowered his head, smelled the ground, and advanced at a very slow walk.

All day he climbed along the rising moorland, pausing now and again to feed upon the heather, or to drink sweet water from the singing streams. With the fall of evening, he passed through a rocky gorge where there were wild goats that stared at him from the brink of a crag. Then there was nothing but a silent emptiness and the vague form of an eagle poised high in the heaven. He reached the summit and found a shelter beneath a ledge of overhanging rock. There he smelled the ground, turned around several times, and then lay down. He rolled over and over, groaning with delight.

Having rolled himself to his content, he came out from the shelter, walked to the brink of the summit, and looked downward. Far away in the hollow, he could see the highroad and the villages where the people lived. Farther away was the sea, racked into towering waves by the wind. Down there was a tumult and uneasiness. On the mountain there was silence and peace.

Then the spirit of the little black ass exulted. He raised his head, opened wide his jaws, and brayed with all his force. His harsh voice, re-echoing through the mysterious rock caverns of the silent wilderness, was triumphant.

FISHING

On a sunny June morning Michael Dillon, a country gentleman of small means and his son, Thomas, an engineering student at the university, home on holidays, were fishing for pollock. This is how they were fishing.

Each had a dried willow rod about three inches round at the butt and tapering to the top slightly. The length of each rod was about six feet. A few fathoms of fishing line was wound on the rod and the fishermen held coiled in their right hands eight fathoms with a hook at the end attached to a snood, a piece of very thin strong line.

They were using strips of raw mackerel as baits. They would cast their coil of line and then as soon as the hook and bait sank a little, they began to haul in the coil again, very slowly.

They were fishing on a square flat limestone promontory that jutted out from a high cliff at the eastern corner of a little cove, that faced the south and the full force of the Atlantic. It was an exposed spot and so jagged on account of the holes the sea had worn in its face that it could be traversed only on rawhide shoes. And even with rawhide shoes it was difficult for any but a young and active man to jump from one spur to another and keep his footing on the moss and the pointed little limpets that grew on the backs of the spurs. At high tide the sea covered the promontory and swelled up a good distance along the grey face of the cliff. But at low tide the promontory was quite clear of water and all around its rim the sea flopped up and down, and the red seaweed that fringed the rock, glistened.

That morning as Dillon and his son stood a few yards apart at the extreme southern point of the promontory, the sea was very calm. The seaweed sparkled in the sun. The black face of the flat, pock-marked rock behind hummed with life, with insects breathing loudly and crawling about in the clefts and holes, as if they were being smothered for want of water and through the heat of the sun and were appealing to the tide to hurry up and return to cover them again. There was lovely calm sonorous music at the point of the promontory, music made by the sea that was wandering back and forth past the point with the movement of the tide. There were gurgling sounds and swishing sounds, sounds of fountains falling in deep pools, and sounds of heavy buffeting, all mingled together in a soothing and sleepy uneven melody. The air was crisp and warm and there was a smell of sea moss being dried by the sun, a pure, healthy, hunger-inspiring smell.

Thomas Dillon was enjoying the smells, the scenery, the music of the sea and the feeling of the summer morning and the warm sun overhead. He languidly tossed out his line, hauled it in, looked at the bait and tossed it out again. All the time he kept inhaling the air deeply through his nose until his chest seemed to be about to burst through his blue sweater, and then letting out the air through his mouth. Sometimes he smiled dreamily, showing his perfect white teeth. He was a well-built, tall, young man, about twenty-three, dressed in white tennis shoes, grey flannel trousers and a blue sweater. His close-cropped fair head was

bare. He had very blue and dreamy eyes and his ears
were red and rather large. He stood with his feet close
together, right on the very brink of the rock, sometimes
leaning forward as if he wanted to sink down into the
sea that ran at his feet and sleep on it.

His father, Michael Dillon, who fished three yards
away on his right was in an altogether different mood.
His lean, bony, long face was set in a desperate scowl,
so that his blue eyes blazed, and his long sharp red nose
seemed in danger of the skin parting on it. The tiniest
germ travelling along the narrow red slit where his lips
joined would find it impossible to enter his mouth,
and his fuzzy grey beard stuck out from under his red
chin and against the white wollen scarf that was coiled
around his neck in an aggressive ill-tempered manner.
A wide-brimmed black soft hat covered his grey head
and a loose brown suit covered the remainder of him,
with raw cowhide shoes on his feet. He said 'Huh'
viciously every time he cast his line and hauled it in
with jerky little movements as if he were trying to trans-
fix a wave with the hook. He had a cold in the head, he
had been fishing for two hours without success, so he was
in a bad temper. And the tide would turn in a few
minutes and he would have to leave the point.

'Did you ever see anything like it?' he bawled, in
a loud angry voice, turning to his son. He was so irritated that he stammered and kept wiping his perfectly
clean and dry left hand on his trousers. 'Not a bite.
Devil damn the bite.'

The son shrugged his shoulders and smiled.

'Oh, what difference does it make?' he said. 'We are
enjoying the air and the scenery and we are getting an
appetite. I could eat a ton this minute. I don't give a
hang if I never get a bite.'

The father curled up his lips contemptuously and
said 'Phew' with the ferocity of a dog snorting at a
rabbit-hole. He stamped on the rock, glared at his son

and cracked his fingers. 'You are a fine specimen!' he shouted. 'You stand there looking at me breaking my heart trying to catch a pollock and then you have the. . . the. . . coolness to turn around and say "Oh what difference does it make?" Here the father tried to imitate his son's softer voice, but he only succeeded in making a kind of screech like a woman.

The son laughed and said nothing.

'It's not for the sake of the pollock,' continued the father, 'no, it doesn't matter a damn about the pollock. I'd be willing to throw the finest pollock I ever caught back again into the sea after I'd caught it. But it's coming up here and spending two hours foolishly without any sport in reward, that vexes me and it would vex you too if ye weren't a now-then-now-then of a fellow. Bah! Be damned to it for a story.'

The father began to swear under his breath and sneezed between oaths. He stood there with his coil of line in his hand as if in doubt whether to cast again or go away. And just at that moment the son got a bite. He was standing facing his father, laughing good-humouredly, with his right side to the sea, carelessly hauling in his line, when a fathom of the line was jerked back out of his hand suddenly.

'I've struck,' cried the son, suddenly getting excited and wheeling around, his hands shaking as they grabbed the taut line, his eyes dancing, his mouth wide open with agitation. He dropped his rod, a pipe fell out of his hip trouser pocket, his white tennis shoe splashed carelessly up to the ankle in a little pool of water on the rock. 'I've struck,' cried the son again, trying to get his line under control and haul in.

'Easy, easy, may the devil devour it for a story,' cried the father, floundering across the three yards of pools and crevices and jagged rocks that separated him from his son. His eyes were starting from his head with excitement. His narrow red tongue was licking his chin, he had it stuck out so far. He fell on his knee at his son's feet and struggling to a standing position again, had to haul at his son's waist.

'Let go,' cried the son. The softness was gone out of his voice and it was hard like his father's.

'Let go, damn it,' he spluttered, staggering on the uneven rock and trying to haul in. 'Don't you see he's getting among the weeds. Keep back.'

'Give me the line, idiot,' cried the father. 'Snakes, alive, what way are you hauling? Don't jerk him,' he shrieked as the son gave a sudden jerk trying to extricate the line from a little spur where it lodged.

The pollock, as usual with pollock, had run with the hook and then suddenly turned and dived to the bottom, just abreast of the rock. Then he bolted straight back through the thick seaweed. The line was entangled in the seaweed. The father began to swear horribly and grabbed at the line.

'You fool, you fool,' he cried, 'd'ye see what you are doing? Why didn't ye play with him? Give me that line or I'll throw ye in after him. Let go or I'll...'

'Oh, have it and be damned to it,' cried the son angrily, letting go the line and stepping backwards.

'Huh,' said the father. Then immediately he forgot his son and his anger. His face shone with pleasure and he moved as cautiously as a cat tracking a mouse. He began to move farther out along the promontory to a half-submerged projection. There was about eighteen inches of water on this projection and red seaweed grew on it too. It was very slippery.

'Do you want to drown yourself?' said the son in an irritated tone. 'Don't go out there.'

'You go home to your mother,' said the old man, gingerly putting his foot on the submerged rocks. 'I'm going the turn him out of those weeds from here. You just wait and see. . . Unless he gets off the hook with another rush. I'll——'

'Look out!' yelled the son suddenly.

It was too late. The sea had swelled up suddenly and the father was up to his waist in water. He tried to balance himself, he said 'Ugh' and then he swore and flopped headlong into the sea. In another moment, he was swimming and spluttering with his grey beard stuck out in front of him and with the hand holding the line and the fishing rod held out awkwardly in front of him as if the fishing rod were a gun he wanted to keep dry.

'Now, what have you done, damn and blast it!' he bawled. 'You've drowned me.'

'Father, father, hold on,' cried the son anxiously. There was a catch in his voice. He stood on the brink of the rock for a moment, shivering slightly, like a dog fearing cold water, and then he dived in. He came up alongside his father and tried to catch him by the arm.

'Keep away, you fool,' spluttered the old man, striking at his son with the rod. 'Get away, man. Don't get entangled in the line. Be off. Be off.' And he beat him on the shoulder with the rod.

The son in his excitement thought his father had gone mad and tried to close with him. And goodness only knows but the two of them might have been drowned had not another wave heaved them up on the submerged rock just then. They lay in a heap grabbing the seaweed. Then they crawled on top.

'I have him yet,' called the father joyously, feeling his line and beginning to haul.

'Oh, blast him,' cried the son shaking his trousers. They were stuck to his thighs like a poultice.

The father paid no heed. He was hauling with his lips bared from his gritted teeth, saying 'Huh' with every pull. At last there was a flop, a splash, and the father was thrown backwards on to his buttocks and a huge pollock, about three foot long, lay between his legs gasping and banging the rock with his triangular tail.

'Oh boys, oh boys,' cried the old man sitting up and

catching the fish by the gills. 'You darling, you were worth getting drowned for. So you were.'

THE ARREST

There was no moon or star shining in the firmament. A grey night light covered the earth following the sunlight of the summer day. Silence and a sultry heat made the mountains terrifying. They looked like mammoth creatures sprawling motionless on the bosom of the earth.

Down the valley Mary Timmins was waiting for her husband. She sat by the kitchen fire knitting. The door was open wide so that she might hear his approach. When a curlew called or when some bog beast uttered a shrill sound she started up, listening.

She had been reared in a lowland village, where the great plains with their luxuriant growth bred sleepy fat people. She was terrified by the loneliness of this mountain fastness, with its fierce people and its weird stillness on a summer night. In her youth when she awoke at night, she heard trains rushing past on the railway and sounds that reminded her of people and peace and company. But here even in daytime, there was always a feeling of mystery and of imminent danger, as if some predatory horde of men were prowling on the mountains, as they used to do of old, according to the legends.

Tonight she had another fear, a premonition of something dreadful going to happen. Her husband had gone to the little town at the mouth of the valley. Whenever he went he came back drunk and that was terrifying in itself. It always terrified her to see his eyes blazing and his whole body trembling with a nervous activity. In the lowlands people laughed a lot and became stupid when drunk but in the mountains drink made people mad.

At last a distant sound reached her. She rushed to the door immediately. It was the sound of a horse's hoofs beating the earth rapidly, a galloping horse. It came from a low hill that rose in front of the house. The dim forms of two cows grazing were visible. Nearer there were two goats standing side by side on a hillock. On the left was her neighbour's house, a long, low, stonewalled house with a zinc roof just like her own. Everything was grey.

The sound approached. Now the noise of wheels mingled with the sound of hoofs. Then a racing horse appeared on the summit of the hill. It dipped immediately. A trap with two men sitting abreast followed it. Their figures were outlined against the sky for a moment. They were bareheaded. Then they dipped.

She uttered an exclamation, blessed herself and rushed back into the kitchen to light the lamp. She had been sitting in the firelight hitherto because she was afraid of the lamplight. Somehow to her timorous mind, it might disclose her existence to those terrrible mountains and the imaginary men prowling on them.

The lamp flared up. Her pretty little round body emerged from the gloom, her cheeks reddened by the light and excitement, her eyes frightened, her white neck trembling, her black hair in a neat mound. The wood fire on the hearth was smouldering in a heap of yellow ashes.

When she got to the door again the horse and the trap

had halted at the gate. The men had descended and were talking excitedly.

'Jim,' she called, 'is that you? What's up?'

'Be silent woman,' her husband called angrily, 'Open the gate Joe. We'll just run her into the barn and leave her there till morning. If ye drive past Ballymore they'll be waiting for ye.'

Mary began to tremble. She was going to call out again but instead, she rushed back into the kitchen and stood trembling in front of the fire with her hands clasped. She heard the gate opening and the horse crossing the yard at a trot. The barn door opened. The horse and trap rumbled in. The door closed again. Then the two men came towards the house rapidly.

'Jim,' she cried again, 'What's up?'

'Nothing much,' cried Jim with a hoarse laugh, 'only the Civic Guard lyin' in Dromolin with his skull split. Divil take him. Come in Joe. This is the last place they'll look for ye.'

The two men entered the kitchen. Timmins was a tall, lithe man, with a laughing handsome face and fair curls that bunched out all round his head from under his yellow cap. His cousin, Joe Sutton, was short and dark, a gloomy, neurotic man with a hooked nose. They were dressed in blue. Sutton had no cap. His hair was caked on his skull with perspiration.

Timmins went up to his wife and kissed her several times, calling her sweet names and laughing. She began to weep on his breast, terrified. Her crying irritated him.

'What are ye crying for?' he said.

'Was it you did it Jim?' she sobbed.

'Course it wasn't,' he laughed, 'it was Joe.'

'Go out into the yard and shout it to the crows.' said Sutton angrily, sitting on a stool by the hearth, wiping blood from his right hand.

'That's all right Joe,' laughed Timmins. 'What's a

blow? Begob I wish I done it meself.'

'God forgive ye Jim,' said Mary, 'is he much hurt?'

Neither replied. Timmins was becoming more thoughtful after the excitement of his arrival and Sutton was in a terribly nervous state. His face contorted and he could not keep still. Mary stood trembling by the table watching the two of them.

'Get us a drop of tea,' said Timmins. 'Hist! What's that? A motor-car, be the holy!'

Both men rushed to the door.

'They're after me,' screamed Sutton, gripping Timmins by the coat lapels. 'Did I kill him Jim? Did I kill him? Speak man. Speak. Will ye hide me Mary? Will ye hide me?'

'Shut up, damn it,' said Timmins. 'Listen. That's they sure enough. God! There they come over the hill.'

'Hadn't he better run across into the bog,' screamed Mary.

'Run, run!' shouted Timmins.

'I'll not run,' yelled Sutton. 'I'll fight. Gimme a weapon. Where's the hatchet?'

He had suddenly become possessed of a fighting frenzy. He dashed around the kitchen looking for the hatchet in every corner. Timmins ran after him trying to hold him. Mary ran out into the yard, waving her hands in the air and screaming for help. A large motor-car came whizzing down the hillside, its head lights blazing. She ran to the gate to meet it. It pulled up suddenly before the gate. Dark figures jumped out immediately and without pausing, vaulted over the gate into the yard.

'Don't go in,' she panted. 'He's got the hatchet and he's going to kill ye.'

'Go ahead,' a tall man said, 'surround the house.' He flashed a torch in her face.

'Who are you?' he said.

'I'm Mary Timmins. Ye'll not take my Jim, Sir?

It's Joe did it. Sure ye won't? For the love of God, sir, ye won't take him.'

Without replying, the police officer dashed past her. Two men and a sergeant were running on ahead. Mary saw their black figures racing forward, their batons in their hands. She saw Sutton emerge from the house, with her husband hanging on to him, both of them shouting. Sutton had the hatchet. Then she turned right round, threw her hands in the air and sank to the ground. She fainted.

When she regained consciousness, she found herself lying on the settle in the kitchen with a neighbour woman rubbing her hand. She opened her eyes for a moment. She saw her husband talking excitedly in the middle of the floor, while several neighbours listened with open mouths. She closed her eyes again.

'It was how Cassidy sent for the Guards,' her husband was saying. 'He has an old grudge against Joe. We were only singing a song in the bar and everybody was as sociable as ye like. Then a Civic Guard came and ordered Joe off the premises. He just raised the bottle and down went the Guard like a log. Right on the skull. I'm going now to see his mother and fix up the bail, if bail there'll be.'

Mary began to pray and as she prayed she could feel the mountains pressing in all around her, with dark shadows on their bulging sides.

Dawn was breaking outside and a multitude of distant birds twittered.

A TIN CAN

There was an old carpenter in our village called Jimmy, who lived alone in a disreputable two-roomed cabin in the middle of a rough, flat crag, away from the other houses. He was a kind, gentle man, but addicted to drink, and during his drinking bouts his mind became unbalanced. These drinking bouts lasted while he had any money, often for weeks at a time, and for a week or so after getting sober, Jimmy went out in silence, avoiding everyone, jumping over a fence when he saw anybody coming, his reddish beard thick with white shavings, his pale face puffed, his loose grey frieze trousers, with the large, black, square patch on the seat, bundled about his waist like a sack.

When I was very little I always ran away in terror when I saw him coming, but later on I grew fond of him. I remember once bringing him a tin can to mend. There was a leakage in the bottom of the can and my mother sent me with it to Jimmy to have a wooden bottom installed. Jimmy was just seen coming over the crags from the town to his cabin, and Big Brigid, who saw him coming, said he appeared to be drunk.

'Take care,' said my mother, 'not to go into his house. Just hand it in at the door and wait. Tell him to hurry. I'll want it for the milk in the evening.'

I arrived on the little green grass plot in the front of Jimmy's door. The door was wide open, and I could hear Jimmy moving about within, grumbling and growling. A dog was whining. There was no window in the kitchen, and the day was misty, so that it was hard to see anything by looking in. I coughed, but Jimmy took no notice. Then I took courage. I went right up to the door and put my head in.

'My mother sent me with this,' I said. 'It wants a new bottom.' Jimmy was at the fireplace putting a tiny pot of potatoes on the fire. He had tea brewing in the ashes in a saucepan. He looked at me angrily, made a snap with his teeth at his beard like a dog trying to catch a fly, swore, and came over to me.

'Give it here,' he growled.

'She wants it for the milk,' I said.

'The devil take the milk,' he said.

I began to get afraid, and jammed my back against the door, with my hands behind my back. The tiny pot, hanging over the fire by an immense pothook, began to emit steam. Jimmy banged the can on his long deal table, that was covered with shavings, carpenter's tools, pieces of plank, a muzzle-loading gun, an oilskin coat, a statue of St. Joseph with one hand off, a loaf of bread, and an alarm clock with the mainspring sticking out behind in a crooked coil. A red cur came in at the door, sniffing, and shivering at every sound. Jimmy, swearing, began to saw away at the bottom of the can.

The cur kept sidling up to the fire. Then he suddenly rushed at the pot and tried to pick out a potato. He yelped as the boiling water touched him, and bolted for the door. Jimmy yelled too, caught the alarm clock, and hurled it out the door after the cur. He hit the cur on the flank with a ding and a rattle. He yelped. I threw myself on the floor and put my fist to my mouth. 'Damn everything,' said Jimmy, going back to the tin can.

While he was sawing away, the cur came in again. Jimmy saw him come in, and dropped his tools. The cur, mad with hunger, took no notice. He trotted boldly down to the hearth, dived at the pot and stuck his snout into it up to the ears. The boiled water scalded him horribly. He yelped and jerked himself away. He brought the pot with him, and the potatoes spilt into the ashes. As he whirled about on the hearth, yelping with pain, he upset the can of tea. A hot steam arose, and a terrible stench of wet ashes, boiling potatoes, and strong stale tea. Then the cur bounded out the door and began to roll himself over and over on the grass.

Jimmy did nothing for five minutes but gape at his ruined meal. Then he silently took the rusty old gun, took deliberate aim at the dog, and fired. The shot went out over my body with a deafening roar. But instead of hitting the dog the charge landed over the door and mortar fell in a shower.

'Tearin' ouns,' yelled Jimmy, 'I missed him,' and began to batter my can with the barrel of the gun. 'I missed him,' he yelled, as he flattened it to a thin plate of tin like tissue paper. Then he hurled the battered thing at me, crying:

'Be off now and see will that hold yer milk, ye. . .'

THE CARESS

With a sudden movement of his arm, Delaney raised his pint and drank, until the stout had sunk into the mass of froth that lay at the bottom of the glass. Then he shuddered and let his arms hang loose, forward from his stooping shoulders, in the attitude of a man beginning to get drunk. The glass canted forward. The froth poured forth on to the earthen floor, where it made a brownish pool, decked with golden bubbles that swelled and burst. He raised his head. His eyes had grown dim and bloodshot.

'I want to marry a young girl,' he cried in a harsh tone. 'I'll have Mary Madigan or nobody at all.'

Pat McDonagh, a tall, handsome man with curly golden hair, sitting opposite Delaney on a low stool, laughed and said:

'Well, that settles it. There's no more to be said.'

'Sure,' said Delaney. 'I'm fifty years of age, but I'm able to make children yet. I want children. If I marry Kate Cody, she's forty if she's a year, where would I get children? She's dry like an old shoe. I want a young girl like Mary Madigan. Come with me, neighbours, in God's name, and ask her for me.'

He began to perspire. Ordinarily a silent and modest fellow, drink had made him garrulous and somewhat repulsive. His cap was at the back of his head, the peak upright from his forehead and to one side. His hair was almost white, yet his face had the innocence and freshness of youth, a sort of virginal expression that looked incongruous for a man of his age. His cheeks were as rosy as those of a young girl. His mouth and nose were well shaped. He had fine eyes. Yet he was dry and withered 'like an old shoe', as he said himself. He was not dry and withered because of his age, but because he had never known the joy and exuberance of passion granted its fulfilment in action. His whole lank body, all hunched and twisted by hard work in the fields, told the same tale of frustration as his face; lean and hungry and unkempt, like a tree whose growth had been arrested by a sudden drought of the earth about its roots. The joints of his big toes bulged out like great thorns through his rawhide shoes.

'Go your own road,' said Dan O'Brien, a squat, powerful man with a bald forehead, who sat beside Delaney on the form, 'though you'd be a wiser man to take my advice and marry Kate Cody. She's yours for the asking. How do you know she can't have children? Nobody has tried her nest for eggs. They may be there in plenty, and chickens too, if she had a good cock on her roost. How do you know you'd have children by Mary Madigan? Look at Pat McDonagh there. He's a fine man and his wife is a neat schooner of a woman, fore an' aft, without a tear in her full rig, but he has no children.'

O'Brien laughed, fondling his pint between his thighs. McDonagh leaned forward and struck him a heavy blow on the chest. The blow resounded, hollow as on a drum.

'Curse you,' said McDonagh, 'you think because you have six sons that you are a better man than me. Change wives and I'll show you. No matter how good the bait

may be, the fisherman comes home empty if there are
no fish.'

O'Brien laughed and pulled McDonagh towards him
by the shoulders. They kissed one another drunkenly
on the cheeks.

'I want to marry a young girl,' cried Delaney once
more. 'Are ye coming with me, neighbours?'

'Yes,' they answered, 'we'll come with you, Bartly.'

'Give me three bottles of whiskey,' Delaney said to
the tavern-keeper.

'Three bottles, you devil,' said O'Brien. 'Is it for the
wedding an' all?'

'Three bottles,' said Delaney. 'It would be only one
if I went after Kate Cody, but Mary Madigan is another
story entirely. I'll show here there's money in my
purse.'

'More power to you,' said McDonagh, nudging
O'Brien.

The two of them winked at one another and giggled
behind their hands while Delaney counted out the
money from his purse. Then each put a bottle under his
jersey and they left the tavern. They turned west along
the road to Portoona. They were all fairly drunk. It was
a summer's evening and there was a fresh breeze blowing
from the sea. The freshness of the air made them dizzy.
They staggered slightly. Delaney began to sing in a
harsh, cracked voice.

'Keep quiet,' said McDonagh, 'or you'll get no wife
to-night, for you'll lie beaten in the barracks.'

'I want to marry a young girl,' Delaney cried.

Then he walked on in silence. He looked ridiculous
in his incipient drunkenness, uttering such a cry. When
he walked, drunk in that way, his premature old age was
more apparent. He was like one of those returned
emigrants one often sees, fellows who worked ten years
or more in American factories that sucked their blood.

Opposite the post-office a young man, who sat on a

wall, saluted McDonagh and said:

'Going home, Pat?'

'Come west with us a bit,' McDonagh said.

'I'm satisfied,' the young man said.

He jumped lightly from the wall and fell into step beside McDonagh. His name was Martin Derrane. For three years he had been serving a soldier and he was now returned to our village, where he lived with his aunt. Although it was nine months since his return and he had long since spent all his money, he showed no inclination to look for work, but talked vaguely of going to America. He was extremely handsome, very slim and dark, with splendid white teeth and eyes of a peculiar intensity.

They were a fine sight, those three young men, all in their prime and fashioned with an elegance which is, alas, much too rare in nature. McDonagh towered above the other two, his golden curls drooping over his forehead. Their arms and legs swung in rhythm and their hips moved from side to side in unison. Their shoulders, held level and rigid, jerked with each step. Women turned in the road to look after them as they marched west, with the red glow of the setting sun upon their bronzed faces.

Delaney, plunging along behind, looked like their servant; and yet, poor man, his thoughts were full of conceit. He felt certain that the beautiful Mary Madigan would be his betrothed before morning.

'Huh!' he muttered to himself. 'They wanted to bring me to Kate Cody's house. She's a good worker, is she? What's that to me? I can do all the work that's needed. I want a young girl between sheets. I want children. I've been long enough a lonely slave of the land.'

They did not speak until they were some distance west of the village. Then they turned into a narrow lane and sat under a fence. Delaney took the bottle from his jersey and drew the cork. They each drank two rounds. The bottle was empty.

'My soul from the devil!' Delaney cried. 'There's one of them gone. Two bottles are not enough for that house.'

'Devil roast you,' McDonagh said. 'Can't you get potheen at the sheebeen?'

'All the same', said O'Brien, 'It's a shame to have a man spend all his money and he maybe not going to get the girl after all.'

'What house are ye heading for?' young Derrane said.

'Madigan's house, you devil,' McDonagh said. 'You should know it well, you young dog, for you're often nosing on that scent.'

Delaney looked suspiciously at young Derrane. Derrane frowned at McDonagh and said in a surly tone:

'Which daughter are ye after? The eldest one, Julia?'

'Julia!' shouted Delaney. 'I'd rather lie with a corpse. No, son. It's Mary I'll bring to the altar. I have thirty acres of land and plenty of stock and money in the bank. So I'll get her. Come, neighbours. Strike the road, in God's name. The night is falling.'

He went in front with O'Brien. Derrane walked in the rear with McDonagh.

'Look here, Pat,' he whispered angrily. 'I'll not go with ye.'

'Why so?' said McDonagh.

'Devil roast his bones!' said Derrane viciously. 'Hasn't he the impudence to cast eyes on the most beautiful girl in the parish?'

'What do we care?' said McDonagh. 'We'll get a good night out of him.'

'Well, I care a lot,' said Derrane. 'I love her. That's why.'

'Then why don't you ask her yourself?'

'How could I? I haven't a penny.'

'What does that matter?' said McDonagh. 'She ought to have money. She was six years in America, earning good wages, and she's a steady girl. Make up to her and take her with you to America. She'll pay your passage if she cares for you. Come on with us, man. To-night is your chance to have a word with her. You can slip out with her into the yard when everybody is drunk and careless. Have sense, man. Sure I'd rather you'd have her than an old devil like Delaney. Aren't you my second cousin, eh?'

'Thanks, Pat,' said Derrane, gripping McDonagh's hand.

They hurried and joined the others. Delaney had now become very garrulous.

'When my mother died last year,' he said, 'I had two hundred pounds in the bank. Now there's only eighty pounds left, but that should last me out until my marriage. When a man is raking round after a wife, he's every scoundrel's pet. Dry mouths and empty pockets gather round him like flies.'

McDonagh nudged Derrane and winked. Derrane scowled.

'Seventy pounds all told it cost me to chase after that young girl from Inishtual,' said Delaney.

'You'd be better off to leave the young girls alone and look for a serious person of your age,' said O'Brien.

'Seventy pounds!' said McDonagh, in a tone of pretended horror. 'It's a fortune for a poor land slave to spend.'

'Seventy pounds in all it cost me,' shouted Delaney, 'and for that much I didn't even squeeze her in my arms. It was robbery.'

'How was it robbery?' said O'Brien. 'You fool, you deserved all you got.'

'All the same,' said Delaney, 'It wasn't fair. I caught sight of her on the steamer going into the town last November and she looked fine; red and juicy like an orange. God! She brought water to my mouth. Her brother and her uncle were with her, so I made up to them, and when we landed, we drank together. John Hernon from my place was there, so I gave him the word while we were at the back of the house and he drew down the talk of marriage. He put it fair and square, how I didn't care for a portion. Thirty acres of land and money saved. What did I want with a girl's portion? Only her flesh and blood and the harvest of her womb. Cripes! The brother and the uncle said they were well satisfied. They said this and that, we drank for days and the money flew. Back I came home from the mainland. I got a boat and a crew and I went to Inishtual with a keg of whiskey. We spent a week on that island and we drank nearly all that was on it, but all the while I never got any nearer to the girl than a goat to Heaven on the Day of Judgment. I came home empty and the tally was seventy pounds.'

'Ah! God help you, poor man,' said McDonagh in mock sorrow. 'Let's sit under this wall and have another drink to drown the memory of what you spent.'

'Let's go on,' said O'Brien. 'We're drunk enough as it is. We can't go footless into Madigan's house.'

Now it was night, but the full moon was up and it was almost as bright as day. They sang an odd stave as they walked, clasping hands and stumbling, one against the other. As they were passing a field close by Portoona strand a young mare put her head over the fence and whinnied.

'That's my little mare,' McDonagh said. 'She's faster on the road than a diving gannet. Let's take her on the strand for a bit. We'd be too early yet at Madigan's house.'

He knocked a gap in the fence and took the mare's halter from beneath a stone. He put it on her head and led her on to the road.

'God! She's lovely!' said O'Brien.

He caressed her haunches. The young mare shivered

as his hand passed gently down her glistening, black
hide. Her wide, silken nostrils twitched and she pawed
the road with her fore hooves, one after the other. Her
long tail lashed her sides. Her head, curved inwards to
her neck by the drawn halter, edged from side to side,
struggling to break loose. Her great eyes looked frightened. She was afraid of these drunken men who
crowded round her, talking in loud tones and staggering.
She sniffed at the strange odour of alcohol from their
breath and felt afraid.

'Get up on her, Pat,' said Derrane. 'We'll see who
can turn her shortest at full gallop on the sand.'

'I'm satisfied.' McDonagh said. 'Hold her head. She's
nervous in the night.'

They held her head and whispered to her. She tried to
rear as McDonagh leaped on her back.

'We have no time to race her on the strand,' grumbled
Delaney. 'They'll be snug in bed before we reach the
house unless we hurry.'

'Have you no shame in you?' said Derrane. 'Can't you
be quiet?'

'You son of a loose mother,' shouted Delaney, 'you
want her yourself.'

He rushed at Derrane with clenched fists. O'Brien
came between them.

'Keep quiet,' he said, 'or I'll beat the two of you.'

They jostled about, the three of them, shouting. The
mare took fright and reared. McDonagh loosed the
halter, touched her on the side of the neck with his
palm and leaned forward over her ears. Then he yelled.

The mare gasped and shot forward like a stone from a
catapult. Her four steel-shod hooves swept from the
hard road with a scraping sound and then you could
only see her tail, spread like a black fan behind her, in
the cloud of sandy dust she raised as she ran west. The
men on the road ceased jostling. They answered McDonagh's yell, excited by the mare's glorious running in the

moonlight. Then they followed her down to the strand.

'Let's not delay here,' said Delaney, when they reached the sand. 'It's time we were at Madigan's house.'

'God's curse on your hurry,' said O'Brien. 'Let's ride this lovely mare first on the sand. Christ in Paradise! No swallow ever drank the wind as fast as she.'

Swinging the long halter about his curly head, McDonagh turned the mare at the far end of the strand and then rode back along the sea's edge where the low tide was frothing gently among the moonlit pebbles. Down there the hooves hardly made a sound and you could hear the mare's breath in the distance, coming in sudden gusts, like the sound a thumping dashboard makes in a full, closed churn. Then she halted, panting, and McDonagh dismounted. The other two gathered round her. Delaney went up near the road and sat on a rock. He felt angry.

'They don't care whether I get her or not,' he said to himself. 'They only want to spend my money and get a good night's drinking out of me.'

As he looked at the three beautiful young men down there on the sand about the dancing mare, all tense with youth's wild energy, carousing in the moonlight by the murmuring sea, he felt enraged at his own impotence. He saw his youth misspent and barren of pleasure, a callow lout who feared to look a woman in the eyes, his widowed mother's pet, looking askance, with brutish disapproval, on all amusement, as temptations of the devil and shameless extravagance. Then his mother died. He was alone. A wife became necessary.

Then for six months he had scoured the island for a bride, unseemly like a rampant goat, which at the fall of autumn goes abroad upon the crags, malodorous, to leap on all and sundry with a wailing cry, in which there is a forecast of bleak death.

'Blood in ounce,' he muttered. 'It took me twenty

years to gather that two hundred pounds and I've spent nearly all of it in six months, making a fool of myself with lads that are only laughing at me.'

He jumped to his feet, suddenly determined to go home and leave them. But immediately he thought of Mary Madigan.

'I'll stay,' he said fiercely. 'When I'm married to her the whole island will see that I am a man as good as ever was bred here. I'll be nobody's fool to be laughed at.'

This thought gave him a wild courage.

'Come on,' he shouted, 'or I'll get better men than ye to come along.'

At that moment young Derrane, mounted on the mare, dashed west along the sand, by the sea's edge, where red weeds were glistening in the moonlight on the white shore. He yelled and swung the halter about his head. Delaney picked up a pebble and threw it savagely after the mare. It fell with a dull thud into the sea.

'Hey!' cried McDonagh. 'What are you throwing stones at?'

'Come on, I say,' shouted Delaney. 'If ye don't want to come, I'll get other men. I have the money. I'm not depending on ye.'

'Devil take your money,' said O'Brien. 'Come down and ride this mare.'

'I don't want your mare,' said Delaney. 'I have a mare of my own. I'll fight the three of you. I'm a man as good as ever was bred on this island. Come on. You're trying to make a fool of me. I'll show you what I am.'

He began to strip off his clothes.

'We had better humour the poor devil,' said O'Brien. 'He's so hot on the scent that he's out of his mind.'

'Devil take him,' said McDonagh. 'We have the two bottles. Let him go if he wants to go.'

'All the same,' said O'Brien, 'Let's humour him. We'll have fun at Madigan's and we might get a gallon of potheen out of him as well.'

'It's more likely we'll get hot water thrown on us, coming with an old ram like that,' said McDonagh.

They tittered and stumbled against one another. They went over to Delaney and took hold of him and flattered him. He struggled in their powerful arms, but he soon grew calm and forgot his anger. Each of them took him by an arm and they marched west with him.

They saw the mare trotting towards them, riderless, with her halter trailing on the sand.

'Blood in ounce!' said McDonagh. 'Martin Derrane is thrown.'

'So he is,' said O'Brien. 'Look at him stretched unconscious over there.'

'Ho! The devil mend him!' said Delaney. 'I'd rather that than two fat bullocks.'

O'Brien began to run towards Derrane. McDonagh caught the mare and pulled her after him.

'I hope he broke his blasted neck,' said Delaney, as he floundered after them through the sand.

They found Derrane stretched limp, face downwards. They raised him and poured some whiskey down his throat. Then he opened his eyes and shook himself.

'Are you hurt?' O'Brien said.

'I'm not hurt,' muttered Derrane.

He struggled to his feet.

'It was how she slipped up in a pool of water when I turned her,' he said. 'She was frightened by the row ye were making and she lost her balance. I'm all right now.'

He began to wipe the sand from his clothes.

'Thank God, there's no harm done,' said McDonagh, examining the mare's legs. 'No. She's all right. Let's go on to Madigan's.'

'There's never harm done when it's needed,' said Delaney.

Derrane looked at him fiercely, but he said nothing.

They walked away. The accident had sobered them a little and they went quietly. When they were near Madigan's house they halted to take counsel.

'Let you begin the talking, Dan,' said Delaney to O'Brien.

'I'm satisfied,' said O'Brien, 'if Pat McDonagh backs me up.'

'I won't let you talk alone,' said McDonagh, 'but it's up to Bartly himself to put in a word with the girl.'

'I'll have a word with her,' cried Delaney, 'and a hold of her too.'

'I'll see you don't,' muttered Derrane.

McDonagh nudged him and whispered:

'Hold your whist, man.'

There was a little pier at the western end of the strand. The shore rose steeply beyond the pier to a line of crumbling cliffs that swept round the western end of the island to the south. The small hamlet of Portoona was built in a hollow some distance west of the pier. When they reached the houses, it seemed as if they were standing beneath a sloping wall, so steeply did the earth rise in the false light to the western horizon, where the sky's rim was pale, catching the reflected shadows from the moonlit rocks.

They tied the mare to the fence in Madigan's yard. A light shone through the kitchen window. They went quietly to the door and O'Brien knocked. After a little while the door was opened.

'God save all here,' O'Brien said, walking into the kitchen.

'You're welcome. You're welcome,' said Mrs. Madigan from the hearth corner. 'Come down here to the fire. Ye just caught us in time, for we are after saying the rosary and we were getting ready for bed. How are you, Pat, asthore? And you, Martin? Is that yourself, Bartly?'

She kept on chatting and smiling as the men sat

down. Although over sixty, she was still handsome, with the tawny face that goes with pale golden hair and gleaming white teeth.

There was a great commotion, for Madigan tried to bring the visitors to the hearth, while they insisted on sitting in remote corners near the dressers and the back door. Madigan, scenting the whiskey under their jerseys, was very excited. A tall, grey-haired man, he had a long, hooked nose like a Turk. Owing to some tumour on his neck, he had to hold his head backwards to one side, like a man mummified in the act of being strangled. This also affected his voice, which was pitched on a very high note, as if he were calling for help to save him from being strangled.

The commotion subsided and there was a few minutes' conversation about the weather. Then O'Brien called for a glass.

'Ah! God bless you,' said Madigan, walking eagerly to the dressers, 'sure it's yourself never comes empty.'

'It's kind father for him to be generous,' Mrs. Madigan said.

'Don't thank me, but Bartly Delaney,' said O'Brien, pulling the bottle from under his jersey. 'It's for him we came.'

Mary Madigan, sitting on the table by the window with a picture-book open on her lap, glanced angrily towards O'Brien. Then she looked towards Delaney and flushed. She was twenty-six, Madigan's youngest child. Although she had been six years in America she had lost none of that fresh, flower-like bloom which is a characteristic of our island women; that impish laughter of the sea-blue eyes, in which nature seems to have en-gemmed a myriad sunbeams and the snow-white silk of the cheeks, on which she paints bright roses that are kept radiant by an innate purity of soul. Mary was tall, full-bosomed and strong-limbed, with a jutting lower lip and thick. brown hair. Her legs dangled from the table

and she kept moving her right thigh back and forth
restlessly. Her shoulder leaned against the wall.

As she glanced angrily at the visitors she seemed to
say:

'How dare you bring this wretched suitor to my
house?'

Her eyes avoided Derrane. He, on the contrary,
could not take his eyes off her face. He sat in a dark
corner by the back door on a small stool. His eyes were
like points of fire in the gloom. Delaney also watched
her furtively. He sat in a form by the dressers, leaning
forward, with his elbows on his knees. His head drooped
and he breathed loudly, just like a tired sheep. Now
and again he raised his eyes and feasted on the sight of
Mary's legs, then on the plump, round thigh that moved
restlessly back and forth beneath the short blue skirt.
Trembling with excitement because of this voluptuous
movement, he looked upwards to her breasts, which
stood out like big cups against their covering of pale
blue silk. Then, overcome by the shame of lust, he
would drop his eyes to the floor and breathe heavily,
like an over-heated sheep, panting under her load of
oily wool.

While O'Brien forced Madigan to drink glass after
glass quickly, McDonagh amused himself by making
pretended advances to Madigan's eldest daughter, Julia.
She stood by the door of the bedroom on the right of
the kitchen, giggling and twisting about as McDonagh
grabbed at her. She was nearly forty and yet no more
sophisticated than a child. She had rough, flaxen hair
and a red face, coarsened by twenty years of hard work
in the fields and on the seashore, where she gathered
weeds for kelp, up to her breasts in the tide like a man.
No suitor had ever cast eyes on the drudge and yet the
poor simpleton longed for love. She twisted about, like
a stroked cat, as the wanton McDonagh thrust at her.

'Leave her alone, you wicked devil,' said Mrs. Madigan, playfully threatening him with the tongs.

Madigan and O'Brien drank nearly all of one bottle between them in a few minutes. Madigan gulped the spirit with great zest and got intoxicated almost immediately. He began to reel about the floor, talking at random.

'I have two daughters here with me,' he said, 'and well I know which one ye came after. The queen of Portoona she's rightly called, God bless her. Ye're not the first band of men that came to this house after her, and some that didn't come sent messengers, but she has her mind made up to go back to New York. Well! Try your luck, men. Try your luck, I say. I'll not hinder ye. I have another daughter as well — Julia, as good a worker as ever rose from her bed at crack of dawn. Aye! And she can stay on her feet until the sun goes down and then give good service in her marriage bed. Make your choice, however, neighbours. I had ten children, but they're all lost to me bar three, between the grave and America. And Mary is going back unless ye can stop her. I had a good boat and I brought her to the midwife's pier in cargo ten times. Two of them in God's Paradise and eight living. Make a drop o' punch for yourself, Kate, my hearty.'

He embraced his wife, who told him laughingly to behave himself. O'Brien emptied the bottle into a mug, which he gave to Mrs. Madigan. She set about making punch. McDonagh gave the third bottle to O'Brien, who passed it round the company. It was soon empty.

'I'll go and get a gallon of potheen,' said Delaney.

'What for?' said Mary sharply. 'I think you have enough drunk! Save your money.'

'Money!' cried Delaney, jumping to his feet. 'What do I care what I spend? I have lashin's of money.'

'Ha! More power to you, Bartly,' cried Madigan.

'Go to bed, father,' said Mary. 'You're drunk. You'll be sick in a minute, same as you were the night that other man came here. I don't want anybody coming here looking for me.'

'What do I care for the other man?' cried Delaney furiously. 'I'm different. I have thirty acres of land and plenty of stock and money saved. I'm as good a worker as ever handled a spade or cast a net over a boat's stern!'

'True for you, Bartly,' said O'Brien.

'True for you,' said Madigan, shaking Delaney by the hand.

'Come with me for a gallon,' cried Delaney.

'You're wasting your money as far as I'm concerned,' said Mary.

'Come with me, Madigan, to the Sheebeen,' cried Delaney, now in a drunken frenzy. 'I'll show you how I can spend money. Let ye drink till morning and I'll pay.'

'Let Pat McDonagh go with you,' said Madigan. 'It would be a shame for me to go, seeing the reason of your visit.'

Delaney and McDonagh left the house. O'Brien took Madigan by the hand and began to praise Delaney:

'You wouldn't get a better husband for your daughter in the whole parish,' he said. 'What does it matter about the colour of his hair? I wish I had a horse the colour of his hair. Your daughter will have a good neighbour, too, for my Kate is next door to Bartly, and a better woman than my Kate never stepped in shoes. For God's sake take advice and make this match, in God's holy name.'

'If I had the say, I'd make it and a thousand welcomes, for either daughter,' cried Madigan, 'but it's herself has the say.'

O'Brien, Madigan and Mrs. Madigan began to talk, all together, holding hands and embracing one another. The punch had gone to Mrs. Madigan's head. They paid no attention to what they said. They were all in that extravagant state of joy which comes from an occasional tipple.

Mary left the table and stood beside Derrane.

'Have you nothing to say?' she said angrily.

Her bosom heaved. Derrane leaned back and stared at her intently. He did not speak, but the muscles of his face and throat were all in motion. One could see that he had been a soldier from the way he held his body, erect from the hips, with the shoulders squared and level, the head correctly poised on the neck. His dark eyes seemed aflame.

'Why did you come here?' she whispered.

'I want to talk to you,' he whispered.

'What is it?'

'Something I want to say.'

'Well! Then say it.'

'I can't here.'

'Why?'

'People are listening.'

She shrugged her shoulders and folded her arms on her bosom. Her shoulders were trembling. They were silent for a little while, staring at one another. The other voices became louder and more unbalanced. Julia crept along the wall, watching the two lovers in the corner and grinning. She suddenly burst out laughing and covered her face with her hands. Mary started and whispered to Derrane.

'Maybe I'll talk to you later outside,' she said. 'I'll try to manage it. Wait outside for me.'

She walked smartly towards Julia, swaying at the hips. Her body looked beautiful in motion. Derrane pursued her with his eyes, greedily. Julia, seeing her sister approach. laughed aloud once more and then ran into the bedroom, clumsily stumbling against the half open door, which she tried to close behind her. Mary, however, was too quick. She forced her way into the bedroom and closed the door. There was a muffled scream and the sounds of hands slapping something soft. The three who were talking loudly by the hearth took no notice. Derrane suddenly jumped to his feet and went out into the yard. There he met Delaney and McDonagh returning with a gallon of potheen in a sack.

'Who's that?' McDonagh said.

Derrane moved away without answering and McDonagh went into the kitchen with Delaney. They put the gallon jar of potheen on the floor near the fire.

'Hoigh! God spare your health,' cried Madigan. 'It's a night till morning now, sure enough.'

'Devil roast the first man that falls,' cried O'Brien.

They began to drink once more, passing the glass rapidly. They coughed as the pale, raw spirit burned their throats and descended to their stomachs like an enraged enemy of reason and conscience. They got to their feet, sat down and rose again without purpose. They sang, shouted, danced, fell on the floor, rolled about and made protestations of their love to one another. There was a tumult as if a band of madmen had broken loose from their confinement and had broached a wine cellar. Mrs. Madigan was almost as tipsy as the men. She ogled Pat McDonagh, who fumbled at her thighs, whenever he staggered towards her in his drunken wanderings. Delaney was the only one who retained a small element of reason. He pursued Madigan about the floor, begging him to talk about the match.

'Bring her here, so that I can ask her,' he kept repeating.

'She's set on America,' Madigan would say. 'Ah! God help you, poor man, she's set on America.'

Tears rolled down his cheeks as he cried:

'I'd rather have you as a son-in-law that a king's eldest son.'

Maudlin with liquor, he embraced Delaney as his best loved friend. He wept aloud and asked God to strike him dead if he didn't love Delaney more than any man on earth.

'Ask her yourself,' he said. 'Try to put the come hither on her with word of mouth.'

'Bring her to me,' cried Delaney. 'Let me get a hold of her and I'll ask her.'

'Drink, you unnatural son of a beggar-woman,' cried O'Brien, 'and don't mind the woman.'

He sat on the floor by the gallon jar and took Mc-Donagh by both hands. They began to sing a song.

'I want to marry your daughter, Madigan,' shouted Delaney, getting furious.

The four of them got to their feet and jostled about the floor. It was hard to say whether they were going to fight or to embrace one another. Then they fell apart, exhausted by this effort. Madigan fell backwards, rolled under the table, sighed and became unconscious in a drunken stupor. O'Brien tried to stay his fall, but failed and fell himself down on the floor. He laughed hysterically and then put his head on his chest and began to sing, waving his hands. McDonagh also sang, with his head in Mrs. Madigan's lap and his hands caressing her old breasts.

Delaney, breathing heavily, like a hot sheep, staggered to the door of the bedroom. He began to knock on the door, swaying backwards and forwards.

'I want to marry a young girl,' he muttered.

Julia laughed within the room. This excited him.

'Who's laughing at me?' he cried. 'Laughing at me? I'll show you.'

Roused by this insult, he seized the door knob and threw open the door. He plunged into the room. In the dim light., he could see the white bed on which a girl was sitting, her arms clasping her knees. It was Julia, but he was too drunk to recognize the difference between her and Mary.

'I have you now,' he cried, plunging towards the bed.

Julia giggled and covered her face with her hands and turned towards the wall. He threw himself on top of her and began to fumble at her body. She struck playfully at him and twisted about, but she did not speak.

Mary had been standing by the door, listening to the people in the kitchen, waiting for an opportunity to leave the house. When Delaney entered she ran into the kitchen. She glanced round the kitchen and then went on tiptoe out into the yard. Derrane was nowhere to be seen. She stood on the stile that led to a path towards the cliffs. She looked all round, but could not see him. Had he gone? She began to tremble.

'Martin,' she called. 'Where are you?'

Suddenly he rose up before her from the earth, like a ghost evoked by her cry. The land sloped sharply downwards from the house, for about two hundred yards, and then it rose abruptly to the left, ending in a cliff, whose topmost point stood against the sea's horizon in the moonlight like a dog's head. To the right, the land continued to descend, gently, to the pier and Portoona strand. The earth here was crusted with flat limestone rocks, lying in narrow rows, like long flat teeth, with lank faded grasses and small briars in the slits. Down in the hollow there were no rocks, except a single massive granite boulder, surrounded by a patch of grass. Derrane had been lying in the shade of this boulder. Now he stood against the horizon of the sea like a mast, dark compared to the grey rocks that gleamed white in the moonlight.

The night was very still. The sea made a lapping sound near by against the cliff, like water at the bottom of a barrel that is trundled. In the distance it simmered on the beach. A faint breeze, lazy and irregular, swayed the pale, uncropped grasses and made the ferns and small briars rustle, like the scraping of mice in a loft, as their tendrils moved back and forth over the surface of the flat rocks. The air was perfumed and so pure that it made the lungs delight in breathing. Oh! So pure that it was hard to believe that sin or pain could exist on this earth.

He waved and she ran towards him. He took her by the hands and led her to the shelter of the boulder. They stood facing one another, their bodies touching, behind the great mass of granite that was taller than their heads. They did not speak, but they both trembled, just like the ferns that trembled at the rock's base under the wind's caress. Her head was bare, and the breeze, playing about her hair, swayed the little tresses that hung loose, so that they rippled back and forth, just like the young blades of grass waving in Spring-time. A long strand drifted over her eyes. She put up her hand to remove it. Then he shuddered and put his arms around her waist. She leaned back and closed her eyes. The moonlight shone on her throat. He began to whisper his love. She groaned and drew her hands slowly down along his body to his waist. Then she laughed and pressed his body close to hers, leaning back from the waist. He gently bared her breasts. They were golden in the moonlight and the dark nipples looked like buds about to burst in Spring with the sun's heat. Then he caressed her breasts and whispered to her, stooping forward slowly, until her waist lay between his widespread thighs and his breath was on her lips. He laid her gently down on the pale, uncropped grass beneath the boulder. She held up the two gleaming bowls of her breasts towards his face and whispered:

'Love me, sweetheart. I belong to you.'

Then he took her unto him and they wantoned on the grass that whispered like fondled silk beneath their leaping bodies. Their cries of love rose into the night like prayers of thanksgiving and of triumph of the divine source of life. The he lay still with his face between her breasts. She caressed his hair and then she put her cheek against his head and sang to him.

Suddenly they heard a shriek. For a moment there was silence and then again the shriek rang out, unseemly on the pure air. They sat up, startled.

'I'll kill the ruffian,' cried a voice.

'My God!' said Mary. 'That's my brother. That's Michael. What's the matter?'

Derrane jumped to his feet and listened. Now many voices shouted in the house. Derrane took a step in that direction, but she caught him by the knee and held him.

'Don't go yet, Martin,' she whispered, rising and clutching him. 'Stay with me. Let's go away together.'

'We can't go now, Mary. Where could we go?'

'Oh! Anywhere. Don't leave me. Take me with you.'

'But where? I have no house. I have no money.'

'Come to America. I have money. Come with me.'

'I'd be ashamed.'

'No. No. You must come. Do you love me? Tell me.'

'I love the ground you walk on.'

'Then you must come. Oh! You must come, Martin.'

'Yes, I'll come.'

'Come to-morrow. No, it's to-day now. Come to-day with me. The steamer comes from the town to-day. It will take us. Will you come to-day?'

'Yes, I'll come,' he whispered, trembling, hardly able to speak. 'Oh! I love you, Mary, but I'm so ashamed, not having a penny. I was ashamed to come and ask your father for you.'

'What does it matter? Only us two. Kiss me.'

The shouting was now louder and they heard a man groan as they kissed. Julia ran shrieking through the yard.

'Don't tell anyone,' said Mary. 'Just get ready and I'll meet you on the pier when the steamer is leaving. Promise me on your soul that you'll be there.'

'On my soul!'

'Say it again, Oh, Martin, I couldn't live without

you another day. I love you so much. You won't go back on me. Say it again.'

'On my soul. Darling! Sure, I'd swim the ocean to come to you. My sweet pulse!'

They embraced wildly and then Derrane stooped and ran towards the pier. With her head thrown back and her hands on her bosom where his head had lain, she looked after him, whispering and laughing. The moon had now grown dim, veiled by the approach of dawn. The sea had turned black, and to the west the land swept upwards in a rigid wall, all black, to the sky, where the dawn mists were gathering, like billowing, grey wreaths.

She ran to her sister, who mer her at the stile.

'What happened, Julia?' she cried.

Julia began to tap her on the bosom, just like a hare struggling impotently in a hound's jaws.

'Michael came home from fishing and caught Bartly Delaney on the bed with me,' she sobbed. 'I think he has killed him. They're all fighting with Michael now.'

'Shut you mouth,' said Mary.

She dragged Julia after her.

'I don't want to go in there,' cried Julia, resisting. 'I'm afraid of Michael. Bartly did nothing to me. Cross my heart he didn't.'

'Shut up, you idiot,' cried Mary.

Julia's rough, grey dress was disarranged and torn at the bosom. Sobbing, she allowed herself to be led into the house.

'What's going on here?' said Mary. 'Be quiet, I say.'

Young Michael Madigan stood against the wall near the back door, struggling to break loose from O'Brien and McDonagh who were holding him.

'Let me go,' he shouted. 'I'll kill him.'

'Be quiet,' said O'Brien. 'Haven't you done enough to him? Try and pacify him, Mary! He won't listen to us.'

Young Madigan's dark eyes looked startled, like a person just awakened from a horrid nightmare. His trousers were flecked with the white scales of fish. His shirt was about his neck and his naked chest was stained with blood from Delaney's face. Delaney lay prostrate on the floor. Blood oozed from a gash in his forehead. His right arm was thrown out far among the bream that had fallen from young Madigan's upturned basket. The silvery sides of the bream and their pink, wedged-shaped tails glistened in the lamplight. Their half-open, dark mouths and their circular eyes, so glassy, seemed to gape at the strange company. The odour of their briny flesh was heavy and almost sickening.

'God help me, I can do nothing to him,' Mrs. Madigan wailed by the hearth. 'Oh, God help me.'

Madigan was sitting on the floor, gesticulating with both hands, but unable to rise.

Mary went over to her brother and said in a low voice:

'Keep quiet, Michael. What are you shouting for?'

He became silent at once.

'Let him go,' she said to O'Brien and McDonagh.

They loosed him. Young Madigan pulled down his shirt.

'What on earth is the matter with you, Michael?' she said.

'I found him in the room with Julia,' cried Michael. 'I'll kill him.'

He was about to rush at Delaney once more, but she pushed him back. Delaney raised his head.

'There isn't a man on the island as good as me,' he shouted. 'Where is the bastard that hit me?'

He pawed the floor with his outstretched hand. The fish began to slip about. He shook his head. The blood flowed down into his eyes. He put up his hand, touched the blood and then looked at it.

'Blood!' he shouted. 'I'm murdered. Who killed me? Where is the murderer?'

He tried to rise but only succeeded in plunging head-long among the fish and the fishing lines which had rolled from the basket.

'Look after him, you two,' Mary said. 'Come into the room with me, Michael.'

She brought her brother into the small bedroom on the left. He sat on the bed and whispered:

'I couldn't help it, Mary. He was pawing at her on the bed and she laughing like an idiot. I wanted to kill him. God forgive me, I'd have killed him only for they stopping me.'

'Was it you cut him?'

'No. I think it was how he fell against the edge of the table when he was trying to make for the door.'

'It doesn't matter, Michael. I'm the cause of all this row, but I'm going away to-morrow, so you can have peace.'

'You're going away to-morrow, Mary?' he whispered, looking at her wistfully. 'Where are you going?'

'No. It's to-day I'm going, Michael. I'm going with Martin.'

'With Martin Derrane?'

'Don't tell anyone, Michael. I'll say I'm just going for a week to the town. Oh, I love him, Michael! You won't be cross with me?'

They put their arms round one another and they began to sob.

'I know he loves you too, Mary, so it's all right, only my father wouldn't hear of him coming for you. I'll come to the town on the steamer with you.'

'I'll always love you, Michael,' she whispered, wiping the tears from her eyes. 'We'll come home when we have enough money saved to buy a farm.'

'I'll always love you too, Mary.'

Again they embraced and wept.

In the kitchen, O'Brien and McDonagh washed the cut on Delaney's head with potheen from the jar. He moaned when the harsh spirit entered the wound. Mrs. Madigan still wailed by the hearth, but she was unable to move. Madigan snored on the floor. Julia crouched over the fish and giggled as she stroked their slippery sides with her finger. Then they raised Delaney to his feet. Julia ran into her bedroom and closed the door. McDonagh poured the remainder of the whiskey into a bottle.

'Well, good night now, and God bless you all,' he said .

'Safe journey to you,' Mary answered from the bedroom.

Nobody else spoke. Delaney's feet dragged along the ground as they led him from the house. As they passed the window of Julia's bedroom she put out her head and whispered:

'Good night, sweetheart.'

Then she giggled and closed the window. O'Brien and McDonagh began to titter. They propped Delaney against the fence where the mare was tied. Then they doubled up with laughter. The mare whinnied and pawed the ground nervously.

'He wanted the young one, but it was the stripper he got,' cried O'Brien, thumping McDonagh in the chest.

'He didn't come away empty in any case,' laughed McDonagh. 'Upon my soul! He's nippy enough when he gets the chance. You couldn't see his tail with dust and he sneaking into Julia's bed. The ruffian should be put in jail for raping the innocent.'

'You're right,' bawled O'Brien. 'He should be cut, the scoundrel. Our wifes are not safe with him about.'

'Ho, the rascal!' said McDonagh. 'If he gets his way. he'll turn the whole parish into a bawdy house.'

Delaney drooped over the fence, his head and arms hanging down the far side. He sickened, as if in answer to their ribald laughter. Then they loaded him on to the mare's back. The mare shivered. She smelt at her strange load and pawed the ground. He lay on her back like a corpse, his head and arms hanging down on one flank, his legs on the other. She smelt one side and then the other. They led her away slowly.

Dawn was breaking as they passed the strand. Curlews were on the wing and their sharp, eerie cries re-echoed in the hollowed cliffs.

Delaney's face looked yellow in the light of dawn. A great blotch of blood had congealed, like red paint on his forehead. His limp carcass looked ever so unseemly against the mare's silken, black hide.

They put the mare in her field and then they sat under the fence to have a drink. Delaney tossed about the field, trying to walk and falling in a heap each time he tried to take a step. The other two paid no heed to him. They drank from their bottle and clasped hands and sang a song of love.

Delaney floundered about the field, muttering:

'I want to marry a young girl. I have thirty acres and plenty of stock and . . . '

It was like a grotesque dance, the drunken leaping of that withered man.

BY THE SAME AUTHOR

The Black Soul

The sea roars dismally round the shores of Inverara.
A Stranger takes a room on the island. Here lives a couple
whose married years have been joyless . . . until the presence
of the Stranger unleashes their passions . . . .
For as spring softens the wild beauty of Inverara, the Stranger
becomes conscious of the dark-haired Mary – how summer
makes her shiver with life. He is the first man she has ever
loved, and she thrills with sexual awakening.
But with autumn comes danger. Peasants mutter superstition
against Mary; Red John laughs at nothing, there's murder in
his eyes; and a madman's yell hurls
the Stranger back to sanity . . . .
Intense, compelling, beautifully descriptive –
as *Wuthering Heights* is to the Yorkshire moors,
so *The Black Soul* is to the Aran Islands.
ISBN 0 86327 478 1

The Wilderness

All efforts to attain happiness and beauty have failed because
we have never known where God is. Outcast Henry Lawless
has retreated into the wilderness – to find him. But the fairy
glen he has chosen has its own laws, invisibly woven into the
apparent calm. Does Patrick Macanasa's tribal claim, hovering
in ever-increasing menace, hold a real threat? Is Eugene
Raverty ready to wield the club of church power against the
newcomer's startling beliefs? Or could the rebellious
sensuality of Mrs Dillon, a symptom of the changing peasant
class, devastate everything?
Stirring the conflicting desires of the glen, Lawless's search
awakes forces ancient and unknown.
ISBN 0 86327 534 6